# TIGER PIT!

Beeker saw a sweeping shaft of light skim the trail before he saw the point man turn the corner. He lay there on his belly, motionless. He was barely breathing, and his eyes were open just enough to see his approaching victim. He held a knife in one hand and the vine in the other—his only weapons against the advancing column of jungle fighters.

Beeker waited until the rear man stepped past; then he pulled the trip wire into place. One after the other, the four men plunged through the leaf-covered top of the tiger trap, clawing at each other in a desperate struggle to avoid the sharpened pungi sticks below. Only two were still alive when the lone black silhouette appeared at the edge of the trap.

Silently, Beeker dropped into the pit with the knife to finish them off.

Other books in the **BLACK BERETS** series:

**DEADLY REUNION**
**COLD VENGEANCE**
**BLACK PALM**

# CONTRACT: WHITE LADY

Mike McCray

A DELL BOOK

Published by
Dell Publishing Co., Inc.
1 Dag Hammarskjold Plaza
New York, New York 10017

Dell ® TM 681510, Dell Publishing Co., Inc.

ISBN: 0-440-11426-8

Printed in the United States of America

First printing—December 1984

This one's for Sandy, who kept me sane,
and Bob, who kept me scared

# 1

It took Beeker a block and a half to realize he was being followed. He knew it from the vague uneasiness in his gut—a gnawing feeling too faint to register. Anyone else would've ignored it. Anyone, that is, who hadn't survived five long years in the deadly jungles between Vietnam and Laos. One thing Beeker learned early in Nam: If you wanted to stay alive five senses weren't enough. The others were the ones that really mattered—the ones most people weren't even aware of. If your gut says someone's following you, you damn well better listen. Beeker listened.

Veering toward the street, he stepped off the curb in mid-block and casually dodged his way through the slow-moving Fifth Avenue traffic. A pretzel vendor on the opposite sidewalk gave him the opportunity to scan the chaotically hustling crowd behind him for possible shadowers. He noted three likely candidates as he paid the skanky-looking character seventy-five cents for a horseshoe-sized ring of semi-solidified cement. The field narrowed to two after he ducked into the front entrance of the F.A.O. Schwarz toy store, with the winner emerging from the store's side entrance about twenty paces behind him.

It's a woman, Beeker noted with impassive surprise. He tracked her slim, jean-clad reflection with his peripheral vision in the glass of the office building on the opposite side of Fifty-eighth Street. Her clothes were properly inconspicuous and her manner just a bit too diffident, but Beeker still couldn't make up his mind about her. She was too eager to be a pro, and too persistent to be an amateur. He had a fairly good idea who she worked for but decided he'd better be sure.

He left-turned onto Madison Avenue, crossed it, and after a block of theatrically exaggerated anxiety—purposeful striding and frequent watch-checking—headed into a handy building entrance. Though he had no way of knowing from the outside, he hoped the lobby would provide him with a setup he could use. He was in luck.

Inside was a bank of four elevators, arranged in two facing rows. Past them on the left was a wide doorway labeled FIRE STAIRS. He slowed his pace to insure the woman following him had entered the lobby, then headed without hesitation through the door. Once out of sight, he soundlessly dropped down the steps leading to the basement. Turning the corner, he pressed himself to the wall and withdrew the nonmetallic Sting fighting knife from its sheath on the outside of his right calf. He held it in readiness, point up at shoulder level, and waited.

For a few seconds no sound came. He visualized her standing there, hand on doorknob in the lobby, the uncertainty playing across her face. She would be debating in her mind: *Should I follow him into the stairway? Have I been lured into a trap?* But he had shown no indication that he knew he was being followed. Was it worth the risk to find out who he was rushing to meet in this building? She decided it was. Cautiously, she pushed open the door.

Beeker watched the stairway's light level increase. He smiled and fingered the glass-reinforced, integrated hilt of his Sting—his social security he liked to call it; ideal for strolling through airport metal detectors without a worry. The woman hesitated long enough to check whether Beeker

10

was lurking behind the door and then stepped through onto the landing. She stood quiet again, listening.

Beeker slowed his breathing to the absolute minimum his body demanded and allowed himself no movement other than a slight widening of his tight, mirthless smile. He knew that if he stayed there, back pressed to the concrete, with his mind clear of all thought save the certainty that he had become part of the wall, she would never know he was there. That was another Nam survival trick. He had become parts of trees, shrubs, rice paddies, hooches, and mud piles more times than he wanted to remember. Never a wall, though. First time for everything, Beeker thought.

As he expected, the woman began up the steps after another short internal discussion. Beeker allowed her three steps before making his move. He was behind her before she could take her fourth, circling her chest with his left arm and pushing the point of the double-edged knife at her neck before she could register any response at all.

"Who?" he asked through clenched teeth. She squirmed helplessly and grunted but otherwise didn't answer.

"Sorry," he said after a moment, "but I'm in no mood to play around." He carved a neat line in her neck from one side to the other, breaking just enough skin to draw blood and cause pain but not enough to do any real damage. An essentially harmless maneuver that as usual proved effective.

"What the hell are you doing?" The woman kicked and bucked in his arms, panic watering her green eyes.

"*Who?*"

"Jesus Christ, are you crazy? Who *what*? And get that damn knife off my neck before you hurt somebody." She was trying to sound unfrightened; she was only partially succeeding. Her amateurishness was showing. Beeker, not feeling particularly patient, prepared to etch another stripe

11

around her petite neck. He got about an inch across before her body went limp in his arms and she stopped fighting him.

"No, I guess you're a no-bullshit type," she said with unashamed resignation. Clearly, the woman had seen the purposelessness of struggle and dropped her innocent bystander act. Beeker couldn't help but be impressed—he liked people who knew when to cut the crap. He moved his knife to a more polite position above the hollow at the base of her neck, and waited.

"The answer to your question is me. I sent you a letter asking you to meet me. My name is Margaret O'Hare."

"O'Hare? You're O'Hare?" Beeker couldn't keep the surprise out of his voice. The woman laughed, obviously enjoying catching him.

"Yes, that was me," she said in a throaty, English-accented voice. "Got you, didn't I?" She laughed again. Beeker's jaw tightened. He didn't like surprises. Who the hell did this woman think she was? She wasn't much more than a kid. What kind of game was she playing? He inched the knife closer to her neck.

"That letter was for real," she went on, suddenly serious again. "I have a job I think you might be interested in." Her eyes, green and unwavering, searched his. Beeker was suddenly aware of the closeness of her body, her small breasts crushed against his left arm, her buttocks jammed close to his thighs, the sourness of her breath mixing with a faint perfume scent. It wasn't altogether unpleasant. . . .

"I don't know what you're talking about." Beeker decided it was his turn to play dumb. He didn't like the way this was going, and perhaps stalling for time would give him the chance to regain control.

"Look," she said with growing exasperation, "my name is Mary Margaret O'Hare, and my father is Major Mike

O'Hare. Perhaps you've heard of him?" Sarcasm was beginning to creep in. "He's also known as the Mad Mick, world's most famous mercenary next to Mr. T. He's retired now, and we've got this company—O'Hare Security Consultants—a sort of referral agency. People come to us with problems, and they pay us lots of money to solve them." She went on. "And *your* name is Billy Leaps Beeker, and you're part Cherokee and a tight-ass Marine sergeant, though it doesn't take a background check to figure that out. You were born on January first, nineteen forty-eight, to a jarhead who died two years later, and his alcoholic wife. You signed up on May twenty-sixth, nineteen sixty-six, and went to Vietnam seven months later. You stayed there for eight years because it was the first time in your life you felt useful. You were sheep-dipped out of the records in sixty-nine and assigned to the Studies and Observation Group, working out of the Forward Operation Center in Danang. You assembled a team, and for the next four years did anything and everything you were told to do—and a lot that you weren't. You did it quite well—so well that you became known as the most effective, and the most dangerous, Black Beret team in the SOG. But that was ten years ago. Most recently you and your team had rather a loud party in the Caribbean. . . ."

Beeker let the woman talk until she ran out of gas. "Remind me to call you when I want my biography written," he said after a few seconds' pause.

"Look," she replied, "can you please let me go now? Standing here with your knife at my throat is not the most comfortable position in the world. Haven't I convinced you yet?"

Beeker let her go and returned his Sting to its sheath. The woman sat down heavily on the steps, pulling a tissue out of her jacket pocket to blot the line of blood welling on her neck.

"Bloody hell. You've scarred me for life."

"I don't like being followed."

"Well, I wouldn't have had to if you'd used the ticket I sent you and checked into the hotel I told you to."

"You can't really expect me to be that stupid. I get a plane ticket in the mail, with a letter signed 'O'Hare' —nothing else—that says you got a job I might be interested in and that I should come talk to you about it. And you expect me to stroll right in, like a hog in a slaughterhouse?"

She laughed again, quickly and openly. "No, if you had used my ticket and hotel reservation I would've written you off. I wanted to see how you'd handle it. But I must say"—she dabbed ruefully at her neck—"I wasn't quite prepared for your style of questioning."

Beeker shrugged unapologetically and turned to leave.

"Wait! Where are you going?" Her hand touched his shoulder.

"Home. Our little game is over."

"Don't you even want to hear my proposition?"

He shook his head. "Not really." Now it was her turn to be confused. Beeker much preferred it this way.

"Please, just listen to me for a moment, okay? It's a very simple, quick job in South America. Minimal preparation, no equipment, low risk, and a *very* generous fee."

"Not interested." Again he turned to leave. She was flabbergasted.

"But this is a piece of cake, Beeker! Don't be a fool! You'll be in and out in less than a week, and no one will even look cross-eyed at you, let alone fire at you. And the client will pay ten thousand a man." Her face betrayed her confidence in the last sentence. Beeker's mask remained firm.

"Well, if it's such a turkey shoot, you'll have no trouble finding a squad of unemployed adventurers to take up your offer. The merc magazine classifieds are full of them." The woman's exasperation was giving way to annoyance, causing Beeker to smile inwardly. He was enjoying this.

"Stop breaking my balls, Beeker! This isn't a bang-bang-shoot-'em-up job I'm talking about. It demands someone with brains and finesse. A team like yours is hard to find."

"Look, Miss O'Hare—"

"Maggie."

"—I don't like any of this. I don't like the way you found out about the New Nuezan business, I don't like the way you contacted me, and I don't like the sound of this job. Nobody offers a team like mine fifty thousand dollars for a no-risk walk-on. You want baby-sitters or muscle, you hire a wrestling tag-team. You come looking for us, then it's risky. Stop trying to bullshit me."

"Then you're interested?" She looked hopeful.

"I didn't say that." Beeker stared her in the face. Sitting there on the step with a bloody tissue in her hand, looking up at him, she looked very vulnerable. Beeker felt his resolve soften.

"Will you at least come to my hotel and listen to the specifics? Honestly, it's a very clean and straightforward job. Let me at least show it to you, and then make up your mind. Doesn't that make sense?" Beeker didn't like the look in her eyes. He felt uncomfortable. She said, "I'm staying at the St. Regis on Fifty-fifth Street." Her eyes said *please*.

To himself, Beeker said, "Shit. Here I go." To the woman, he grunted, "Tomorrow. One o'clock." Then

15

he turned and left her sitting there on the steps, her hand still holding the bloody tissue to the cut he'd put in her pretty neck. As he walked away, he prayed to God she wouldn't call out "Thanks" after him. If she did he didn't hear it.

# 2

On the day Beeker found the letter in his mailbox, he could almost feel Woodrow Wilson Parkes reaching up out of the grave to get him.

He had held the single sheet of paper folded around an airline ticket in his hand and looked at it. He had read the pitch, noted the name "O'Hare" typed in at the bottom of the "OSC, Ltd." letterhead, and had known instantly that merely killing the bastard wouldn't be enough to finish his business with Parkes.

He had been back from Africa for less than a month, and the memory of that final moment with the man who had betrayed him and his team still burned fresh in his gut. He could still see the sweat collecting on the pale skin of the ex-CIA man's pudgy face, his watery blue eyes staring fearfully at the business end of Beeker's .45 automatic. He could still hear the man's wheedling voice and feel the checkered wood handgrip of the Marine-issue Colt Mark IV in his palm, already moist from his sweat. The trigger responded easily to his steady squeeze. . . .

Putting that slug dead-center in Parkes's forehead was the closest Beeker had ever come to really enjoying killing a man. This one had deserved it—in spades. He had lured Beeker and his Black Berets out of (admittedly unhappy) retirement with lies and false promises, sending them back into the Laotian jungle thinking they were rescuing eigh-

17

teen comrades held in a Communist prison camp. But there hadn't been any prisoners, and no prison camp. Every word out of the bastard's mouth had been a lie, and Beeker still hadn't forgiven himself for not expecting this. He knew better than to trust the word of their ex-control officer.

*He should have known*.

But he had swallowed the story because he *wanted* it to be true, and led his men into a near-fatal trap. What they thought was an Agency-approved rescue of a handful of newly discovered POWs turned out to be a local drug-war mop-up. The "prison camp" was an opium plantation, and the "Pathet Lao" guards falling before their bullets were actually local growers tired of taking orders from— and passing all the profits to—absentee landlords: Parkes and his corrupt crew of retired CIA bloodsuckers.

But they got Parkes. First they ransacked the money-stuffed safe in the basement of the plantation house. That felt good. For a while. But Parkes hadn't given up. He had sent men to Beeker's Louisiana retreat—now the Black Berets' home base—to let them know he wasn't the forgiving type. They'd burned down the farmhouse that Beeker had built with his own hands and had almost killed Tsali, the young Indian boy the Black Berets had unoffically adopted as their own. But Tsali had proven himself a man that day; and more, a warrior. The deadly, unhesitating accuracy of the mute boy's bow spoke more of his courage and spiritual strength than words ever could. Beeker had felt as proud as any father on the day his son reached manhood—as any Cherokee brave on his son's return from his first solo hunt. Beeker's pride had been overwhelmed only by his hatred for Parkes and the driving thirst for the blood-sweet taste of revenge.

They'd tracked Parkes to Libya, where he'd set up training camp for mercenary terrorists poised—at his command—to invade a poorly defended neighboring country. The patsy prince he'd lined up to take over in Bashi couldn't run a car wash, much less a country. Parkes had certainly engineered one hell of a setup for himself. If nothing else, he was as ruthlessly resourceful as he was ambitious.

But the Black Berets had kicked that sweetheart setup to pieces. They'd forcibly retired several hundred low-lifes who were on their way to "liberate" Bashi, jiggling seismographs in a thousand-mile radius as proof of their on-the-job enthusiasm.

Then they'd caught up with Parkes at last, sitting on his fat ass, safe in a Bashi villa. He had looked to Beeker much the same as he'd looked in Vietnam ten years earlier. Just fatter and sweatier. Beeker had thought he would luxuriate in the painful death of a man who had betrayed everyone and everything. But he had felt nothing as he pointed the Colt Government .45 and punched a hole in the man's head with it. No more satisfying than killing a field rat. Only after he had turned his back on the splayed corpse and walked away did he begin to feel some of the weight of his hatred lifting.

The letter had brought all this history back to him like a jab in the stomach. There had been no doubt in Beeker's mind where the thing had come from. Parkes might be dead, but the Prometheus Corp.—the shadow-world organization Parkes and his covert-action cronies had set up after they were booted from the CIA—still lived. It had handled their Southeast Asian drug business, their terrorist training business, their arms peddling to any strutting strongman or dubious revolutionary group that came across with the cash, and God knew what else. Now Prometheus was in the revenge business, and the Black Berets were the target. They couldn't get to them on the farm—the place had been turned into a near-impregnable fortress since the last attempt—so they were trying to lure them out. Beeker had shrugged. It was just as well with him. He'd take them on anywhere. *And* whip their chair-flattened asses. No doubt.

Beeker had known, though, that he had to handle this one alone. It had been his fault that Parkes had sucked them back in to begin with—never mind that not one of his men had to be dragged. He should've known that Parkes's word wasn't worth possum shit. Billy Leaps felt responsible; he'd almost gotten them killed, so it was up to him alone to even things out.

He had told no one about the letter. Considering none of the others had been around when it arrived, that hadn't been hard. They were still working their ''vacation trip'' out of their systems, spending money and raising hell: Applebaum and Harry the Greek in New Orleans; Rosie Boone in Tijuana; and Cowboy somewhere in southern Mexico with one of his wives. Only Tsali and Beeker had been on the farm; Billy Leaps because he preferred the solitude of the North Louisiana woods to any crowded, noisy city, and the mute Indian boy because he had become almost surgically attached to the new computer in the main building. He'd almost had to beat the kid's head in to get his attention and tell him he was going away for a while. He'd also given him a sealed envelope with the number of the hotel he'd be staying at in New York, with instructions not to open it unless there was some emergency. The boy could use his computer to contact any, or all, of the team. He'd then made his own arrangements to fly to New York—going into Newark after changing airlines (and names) in Atlanta, instead of using the ticket directly into LaGuardia—packed an overnight bag, and headed out.

Everything seemed different now. Beeker sat in his hotel room overlooking Lincoln Center and pondered his encounter with Maggie O'Hare—if that really was her name—earlier that afternoon. Could what she said have been the truth? He had, of course, heard of Major Mike O'Hare—the Mad Mick—whose exploits in Africa during the last two decades had become part of merc mythology. Commander of the legendary Bush Buzzards in the 1964 Congolese Civil War; later military adviser to Biafra's Colonel Odumegwu Ojukwu; fighting the Cubans in Angola in 1975; then Rhodesia; and finally, some unpleasant business in Namibia. . . .

Beeker knew that much, but did the old guy have a daughter? And did they have a "Security Consultants" operation? Sounded like crap to him. He would have to do some checking. The first long-distance call he made went to a whorehouse in New Orleans. He told the young black girl who answered to give Applebaum his phone number and that it was urgent he call back within a few hours. He knew that the Runt had built up some pretty good merc contacts after kicking around Africa in '76 and '77, on the rebound from Vietnam. He next called some ex-Marine buddies in Alexandria, Virginia, and asked them to find out what they could. The last call went to a phone machine in MacLean, Virginia, where his innocuous-sounding message told someone a phone number and the exact time to call it. In about three and a half hours, Beeker would be in a phone booth on Broadway he had picked out earlier. The phone would ring, and from somewhere in the world, a breathy, seductive voice would whisper in his ear.

Delilah. Beeker hoped she could give him some information, as she had before. The organization that she worked for (if it had a name he didn't know it) existed in the same Twilight Zone as Parkes's Prometheus Corp. They fought a kind of war that Beeker didn't much understand. He knew the night-and-day varieties of war well enough, but it was the region between that confused him, where peace

21

meant covert action, diplomacy meant treachery, and smiling faces talking of "detente" concealed poison-tipped umbrellas and clouds that rained yellow death on mountain tribesmen. That was Delilah's world, and she could have it. But her voice, the touch of her body, and her scent . . . it all did something to Beeker that he couldn't control.

"Hello, Billy. February's a lousy time to be in New York." She sounded far away. It was probably warm and sunny where she was. Beeker shifted uncomfortably in the phone booth.

"I needed a break from the farm," he said to her.

"I could meet you there in a couple of days if you like."

He hesitated. "I think I've had enough already. Don't know why I came. Can't stand this place. An insane city for insane people. No wonder they're always shooting at each other."

"Why'd you call?"

"I hoped you could answer a question."

"Ask."

"What do you know about an outfit called O'Hare Security Consultants, principals named Major Mike O'Hare and daughter Margaret. Are they for real?"

It was her turn to pause. Beeker heard nothing but the whoosh and static of a thousand-mile telephone connection, and some faint, unintelligible leakage from other conversations.

"Yes, they're for real. Why d'you want to know?" Her voice had changed, suddenly becoming cold and suspicious. It was as though Beeker could hear her guard drop into place like a steel door.

"Business," was all he said.

"They offering you work?"

Beeker wasn't sure what he should tell her. Caution won out. "Not sure yet. Just thought I'd check around a bit."

"Right," she said sarcastically. Then serious: "Don't do it, Beeker. It won't be worth it, believe me. It'll just make things difficult for you."

"Nothing's been said yet."

"Don't even listen. Go home. If you need work I'll find something for you to do for us. I thought we had an exclusive."

"That's news to me." Beeker was beginning to feel annoyance at her tone. Like he was a wayward schoolboy or something.

"It'd be much better that way, Beeker. Better for all of us." Was that a threat in her voice?

"Screw you, Delilah. You fucking spooks are all the same— you think you own people. Well, you can forget it. We're free agents, and we're gonna do what we goddamn please."

"Billy, wait—"

He didn't.

Applebaum called him about forty-five minutes later. Beeker had been doing sit-ups on the floor of his room to work off some tension. Applebaum was crotch-deep in Mardis Gras and feeling no pain.

"Beek, you old squaw-squeezer! What the fuck you doing in New York? You should be *here*, man—there's more hungry snatch walking these sidewalks than you ever saw on Tu Do Street. And it's all *free*!" The noise of serious partying in the background was loud enough to almost drown out Applebaum's voice.

"Marty, this is business, okay? Turn off the party glands for a minute. I want you to answer some questions for me." Applebaum grumbled a little bit and made some remarks about the genetic inability of American Indians or Marines to have fun. Beeker ignored him. "What can you tell me about O'Hare?"

"The Mad Mick? He's number one—the best—the generalissimo. Why do you ask?"

"What's he doing now?"

Applebaum thought for a second. "I remember something about a legitimate operation in Europe, security or something."

"Does he have any kids?"

Another pause. "Yeah, one bitch of a daughter named Maggie. Foxy little redhead with a set of tungsten-steel balls. We were, um, quite friendly for a time." Applebaum's innuendo was clear, but Beeker doubted if the truth bore much relation to what the Runt was hinting at.

"Yeah, funny thing about that, Marty. I hear she's a dyke now. You must've ruined her for life."

"Nah, she just realized it would be all downhill from me, so why bother disappointing herself?" As always, Applebaum laughed with hyenalike enthusiasm at his own joke. As always, he laughed alone.

The last call of the night came from Beeker's Marine buddies in Virginia. What they said added no real new information but confirmed what he'd already been told. Every indication was that the woman he'd met on the street this afternoon was for real, that this job she said she had for him was probably just that, a job. He lay in the too-soft hotel bed for a while, considering whether he wanted to hear the details of this alleged job. He didn't really, until Delilah's proprietary tone over the phone came back to him. That helped make up his mind. He reached for the phone to arrange a meeting for tomorrow.

Maggie O'Hare was staying at the St. Regis, on Fifty-fifth Street off Fifth Avenue. Beeker walked there from his hotel despite the cold and was dialing her room number on the house phone at the appointed hour of one.

Upstairs, Maggie opened the door after one knock. She

24

smiled and stepped aside for him to come in, but Beeker only nodded and walked past her. It was a typical New York City hotel room; better furnished than most, but no larger than what Beeker would consider a good-size walk-in closet. The wallpaper was flowered but softly colored, and only offensive if you looked at it closely. In the far corner was a color TV tuned to a soap opera with the sound off. Next to it were two armchairs with a low table between them. Sitting in one of the chairs was another woman. She stood up as Beeker looked at her.

"I'm glad you changed your mind," said Maggie's voice from behind him. She shut the door and brought up another chair. "Do have a seat. I've ordered us up some cold meats for lunch. I hope you'll have some." Beeker, sitting himself in the offered chair and still studying the other woman's face, said nothing. The stranger was annoyingly familiar, and he was trying to figure out who she was. Her hair was blond, brushed back from her face and cut severely at the shoulders. Her face was pretty, in a hard-edged and totally anonymous way, and her blue eyes had a touch of red around the lids. Her nose bore the smooth, shiny texture of cosmetic surgery. She was the kind of woman most men found attractive, but stirred only indifference in Beeker. He would have walked right past her on the street—except that he had seen her before.

"Jackie, this is Billy Leaps Beeker. I think he's our man. Billy, this is Jacqueline Simmons. She's Senior Foreign Correspondent for the Cable News Channel. You've probably seen her on television."

Indeed he had. Jackie Simmons was a flamboyant TV reporter who jetted around to all the world's hot spots, beaming back in-the-maelstrom coverage for the nation's largest twenty-four-hour cable news service. Beeker had caught her act dozens of times—standing solemnly before a bombed-out refugee camp outside of Beirut, speaking

25

glibly and knowledgeably about the situation, a tone of conspicuous sympathy for the costs of human suffering always in her voice.

"I'm very happy to meet you, Mr. Beeker." She flashed him some teeth. "And I'm especially glad you'll be helping us out." More teeth.

"I haven't agreed to help anybody yet. I'm just here to listen." Beeker kept his teeth to himself.

"Of course," she said uncomfortably, trying unsuccessfully to sound humbled. "I didn't mean to presume—"

"Maybe you should outline the job for me, and we can all find out who's going to help who." The women smiled nervously while Maggie took out a cigarette and lit it. Beeker sat back and waited.

"Well, about three months ago," Jackie Simmons started, "my network was approached by a young South American man who claimed to represent certain political interests in his country. He offered us exclusive access to an incredible story and specifically requested that I go to his country to cover it. The story is *big*, and it could very well bring down the government and perhaps a few other things along with it. We need some men to take me and my crew in to do the story and then get us out again, alive."

Maggie broke in at this point. "Quick in, quick out. A few days, maybe a week at the most. And, quite possibly, you won't have to flex your muscles at all. Just be there."

Jackie Simmons studied Beeker's eyes for some sign of what he was thinking, but his mask was impenetrable. Inside he wanted to laugh. Right, he thought. Just be there. Aloud, he asked without expression, "What country are we talking about?"

"Peru." Simmons answered him. Beeker rustled through his memory to see what he could find.

"Didn't they have a military coup recently?" He had a

26

vague memory of some general yanking power from an economically floundering socialist democracy.

"Yes, about six months ago the Defense Minister, a General José Arroyo, surrounded the Presidential Palace one morning and forced President Fernando Belasco Torio to resign—for the second time, the poor man. The military and Presidente have traded places with each other a couple of times since the mid-sixties. This latest coup was ostensibly about the economy, which, like most third-world countries, has been in trouble since about eighty, eighty-one or so. Supposedly, Arroyo took power in order to tighten the government's grip on the economy, but the man who contacted us says he can prove differently. He's told us that he has evidence of a massive conspiracy involving Arroyo, the local and totally corrupt CIA station chief—a man named Pomeroy— and local organized-crime drug interests. Our source says that these men conspired to boost Arroyo into power because he is more tolerant of the drug trade—cocaine is a billion-dollar-a-year industry in Peru. President Torio apparently was actively trying to stop the coke trade, and he was ruining the economy doing it. Arroyo allows it to flourish, and suddenly the country is solvent again."

"Why do we have to go down there to get the evidence? And why do *you* have to go? If he contacted you here, why couldn't he have just brought this supposed documentation with him?" As he had expected, Beeker didn't much like the sound of this. It seemed to him that Simmons wanted to do a bit of journalistic showboating and take the Black Berets along for some camo-fatigue window-dressing.

"Because that's only half the story, Billy," Jackie Simmons assured him. So they were on a first-name basis now, were they? Beeker didn't want to know this woman—would rather be a stranger. She continued the story.

"The other half is Ramón Guiterrez, who leads the reformist rebel forces. He wants me down there to interview him so he can tell the truth directly to the American people. He needs our help, and that's what he wants in exchange for this story. Guiterrez is an honest man, and he should be his country's next president. He *will* be if this story's ever told—and we've got to make sure it is."

"Is this where we all get up and sing 'God Bless America'?" Beeker couldn't believe she was taking all that stuff seriously. He had never met a politician who wasn't a corrupt, greedy coward, and there was no reason to believe that this Guiterrez character would be any different. This good guy vs. bad guy stuff was strictly Disneyland—anyone who knew the way the world really worked could see that. The woman had been doing TV news for too damn long, Beeker thought. Obviously she was starting to believe her own bullshit. Not surprisingly, his sarcasm was coolly received.

"Look, Mr. Beeker"—Billy smiled at the reversion to formal terms—"I don't much care what your politics are. I'm buying your *protection*, not your endorsement. I would therefore request that you keep your cynical wisecracks to yourself. A man who does the sort of work you do can ill-afford moralistic judgments about the motives of others." She ended her speech with a self-satisfied smirk, like a kindergarten teacher who's just told a kid why he shouldn't play with himself.

"Stuff it, Jackie," Beeker came back, staring at her full in the face. "It's doing the sort of work I do that entitles me to take just such judgments. Good soldiers put their asses on the line for what they believe, and if they want to survive, they can't lie to themselves—or to each other. We know who calls the shots, and we know how to get things done. Everything else is bullshit." He stood up. "So, if you'll excuse me, I'll leave so we can stop wasting each other's time." He turned toward the door.

"Oh, sit down and shut up, Billy," Maggie said with mock-sternness. "And stop being such a tightass, Jackie. Both of you drop the games and let's get this business settled. Why don't—" She was interrupted by a knock at the door. She said, "That must be our food," as she went to answer it.

Beeker remained standing as Maggie opened the door. She stepped aside as a cart covered with food rolled in. Two waiters in ill-fitting white uniforms followed it. *Two* waiters? Beeker didn't like the way they cased the room as they entered. Alarms went off in his head. When the one by the door reached for something under his jacket, Beeker went to work. He yanked Jackie Simmons's arm, pulling her from the chair, and threw her behind the bed. "Stay there!" he said through his teeth.

The "waiters" were caught by surprise—obviously they figured *they'd* be the ones doing the surprising. But they hadn't figured on Beeker. They hesitated for an instant, and by the time they went for their guns, it was already too late.

Beeker was trampolining across the bed as the front man reached under a towel. He came out with a blue-gray Browning Hi-Power, enlarged by a hot-dog-sized sound-suppressor. Billy hit him, left hand palm-up into the man's face, right hand clamping the wrist of his gun hand, body taking out the food cart. Cold meat flew everywhere as the cart went over, pinning the man against the bureau. The heel of Beeker's palm caught the man's nose hard, pushing his head backward. He squealed at the impact and immediately started breathing funny. He flailed his left hand in a futile attempt to defend himself, and—panicking—squeezed off a shot from his Browning. The TV set exploded, and

Jackie screamed. Beeker tore the automatic from the man's grip and hit his nose again, harder. The funny breathing got funnier. Beeker grabbed a handful of Brillo-like blond hair and pulled the man away from the bureau. He staggered clumsily and came forward, waving his arms, face reddening. Billy gave one last tug and let go, moving aside for the falling body like a bullfighter. The man's head went into the already broken TV screen clear up to his shoulders. Sparks flew, and the body twitched.

Billy's attention was drawn by the sounds of struggling by the door. Maggie was playing piggyback with the other killer. Her legs rode the man's hips, her arms grappled his, and she was tearing at his left ear with her teeth. Her lips and chin were smeared with blood, and it looked like she was smiling. The man's face showed horrified frustration as he watched Beeker raise the silenced Hi-Power to firing position. The assassin struggled furiously to break Maggie's grip and reach for something inside his jacket—obviously a pistol. He knew he didn't have a chance.

"Duck and close your eyes!" Beeker shouted at Maggie as he extended his right arm, steadying it at the wrist with his left. She took one last pull on the man's hamburgered ear and then did as she was told.

Beeker crouched low, firing up into the man's face. He squeezed once on the trigger, and it was all over. A neat nickel-sized hole opened on the man's forehead. A bigger, messier one opened in the back, his face went slack, and he took two spasmodic, staggering steps backward, smashing Maggie into the red-splattered closed door.

"Ouch," she said, and let the man fall to the floor. She still had that strange smile on her blood-smeared face. Bright red splashes of blood covered her right shoulder.

Billy lowered the gun and exhaled raggedly, letting the tension flow from his body. Jackie Simmons screamed hysterically from under the bed.

"Oh, shut up, Jackie. It's all over," Maggie said.

# 3

"What the hell are you laughing at, Big Chief Hot Shit?"

Beeker caught his breath. "I'm sorry, Maggie—you just looked so damn funny riding the guy like that, having his ear for lunch. I almost wished I had a camera there instead of the pistol. 'O'Hara Chews Attacker to Death.' Don't you think that'd make a great headline, Jackie?"

Jackie Simmons was in no mood to appreciate a joke. She sat on the edge of the bed with her head in her hands, sobbing uncontrollably. Maggie was standing over her, waiting for the woman to calm down. She was holding out a half-filled glass of water, urging Jackie to take it. She had done a hasty job cleaning her face in the bathroom, so some streaks of blood still remained. It looked like messily applied lipstick. Her shirt was beginning to dry.

Maggie grinned and shrugged. "I couldn't come up with a more graceful way of stopping him. Next time I'll take a few minutes out and think up something more . . . ladylike." She laughed.

"How can the two of you joke about this—act like nothing's happened! We were almost killed!" Jackie could barely get out the words between gasping sobs. Maggie and Billy exchanged unsympathetic looks.

"Yes, well, given the choice," Maggie answered coolly, "I'd rather laugh than cry. Don't you agree, Mr. Beeker?"

"Affirmative, Ms. O'Hare."

"Oh—you two are animals! You're killers! You murder two men, then you laugh about it!"

"Now, just hold it a second, Jackie," Maggie broke in. "Who in bloody hell do you think came here to murder who? You've got things crossed—those hoodlums tried to kill *us*, remember? You've heard the expression 'kill or be killed,' haven't you? Well, the man who said that knew what he was talking about." Jackie responded only by continuing to cry. Maggie turned to Beeker and rolled her eyes theatrically. He grinned in reply.

By this time the man with his head in the TV had stopped twitching. Beeker presumed he'd pushed his last room-service cart and, after unplugging the TV set, pulled him from his almost comical death pose. He studied the man's face momentarily, enough to convince himself he'd never seen it before. The jagged glass of the television screen had slashed it a bit, but the heavy features and thick, kinky blond hair were distinctly unfamiliar to him. Taking the poor schmuck by his feet, he dragged him into the bathroom and dumped him in the tub. The second corpse was a bit messier but no more familiar. Blood was leaking steadily from the third eye-hole poked through his skull by the Hi-Power's 9mm slug. Beeker relieved the man of his weapon, a brand-new .22 caliber Beretta 70S, with the thumb safety catch still engaged. It had the lubricant smell of an unfired weapon, and Beeker wondered if the man had ever gotten to squeeze the trigger. Probably not. No matter; he was now half the dead meat in a hotel-room bathtub.

"Any idea who those two were?" Beeker asked Maggie as he emerged from the bathroom, wiping his hands on a towel.

She shrugged. "Not specifically. They're both strangers, but I presume they've something to do with this Peruvian business." She glanced at Jackie, who had downshifted

33

from sobbing to whimpering. "Something tells me this isn't going to be the harmless joyride we're trying to convince ourselves it'll be."

"I knew that yesterday," Beeker said, trying not to sound too much like he was saying "I told you so," which was exactly the way he felt. He tossed the towel through the bathroom door and then settled himself in one of the chairs by the window, propping his legs on the temperature control unit. He addressed himself to Jackie, whose whimpering had segued into a nearly tolerable sniffling.

"You've got to understand something very important about this sort of job, Jackie." She looked up at him pathetically, red eyes squinting. "This isn't going to be just another breeze-in-breeze-out afternoon taping. Lots of people don't want us going where we'll be going—lots of *heavy* people. A billion dollars carries a lot of weight. You saw what just happened here, right? Well, that's only the beginning. There'll be more, *lots* more and *lots* uglier. If you can't take a little shooting, then we'll all be dead in twenty-four hours. I want you to think about that long and hard before you even pack a toothbrush."

Maggie laughed. "When did you decide to go?"

"Well, I must be nuts, but I don't much like it when two shit-for-brains try to take me out—*before* I've even decided to take the job. Pisses me off; makes it seem like I don't have a say in the matter. So, hell, if I'm going to take the heat for a job, I might as well do the damn thing and get paid for it. I don't fancy the idea of dying for something I've turned down."

Maggie shot him a crooked grin. "I suppose there's some logic to that—however twisted it might be. I'm glad you're going to do it, though, whatever your reasoning."

"I've got some conditions, though. They must be met before we'll go."

"Like what?" That last statement stirred Jackie into

finally speaking. She had almost returned to her self-possessed, unflappable, TV-image self. Almost.

"First of all, forget the fifty thousand. Double it, and add Maggie's fee on top."

Her eyes narrowed. "I guess they don't call you people mercenaries for nothing."

Maggie stifled a laugh. Beeker ignored her. "If you want in to this country and then out again with your scalp intact, a hundred thousand is cheap. And not only because we're greedy—we'll be needing some equipment, either brought in quietly or purchased locally."

"Do you mean guns? Is that the equipment you're referring to? But we've been guaranteed protection by Guiterrez and his men. We won't need any guns."

Beeker shook his head. "Sorry. The Black Berets look after their own asses. And *you'll* be our responsibility as well. We trust no one else to handle our responsibilities. Ever. We'll need equipment." He said the last sentence with an unmistakable finality, denoting: "Case closed, no argument." There wasn't any. He continued, "Besides, I want to squeeze blood out of your boss's wallet. I want to hear him yelp."

Maggie giggled at Beeker's reference to Tom Tyler, the well-known owner of the Cable News Channel—an obnoxious Florida businessman who acted like he had more mouth than brains.

"Beeker," she said with affection, "I think I'm going to enjoy working with you."

Beeker continued with his countdown, letting a smile reach his eyes but not his mouth. "Next, we can forget this me-and-my-crew shit. There's no way we're taking anyone else in but you. Me or one of my men will handle any videotaping there is to be done—extra human baggage will just make the whole thing more difficut. Hell, I'd leave *you* behind if I could, but it looks like we're stuck with that part of the deal.''

"Is that all, Mr. Beeker?'' Her eyes, all trace of crying gone, were pure, smoking dry ice.

"No,'' he answered her, unperturbed. "Most importantly, *I* am in charge. Completely. You are to listen to *everything* I say, obey *every* command I give, without thinking, whether you like it or not. Your survival depends on it. Is that understood?''

Her only answer was a cold, stony glare. Beeker tried again, introducing a spark of menace to his delivery.

"I said, is that *understood*?'' This time she nodded her affirmation. "Good. And if you want to live, you'll make damn sure you don't forget it.''

Silence.

Billy shifted himself to a more comfortable position in the chair, locking his fingers behind his head as if he were holding it in a catapult sling, ready to shoot the thing off his neck and out the window onto Fifth Avenue below. He flexed his neck backward two or three times, and pushed his chin forward in a pointerlike gesture. The women watched him in silence.

"What sort of a timetable are we operating on?''

"That's up to you,'' Jackie answered. "As soon as you're ready to go, we'll go. Guiterrez doesn't know how much longer he can stay alive under present conditions. The U.S.-supplied government troops are pushing him farther into the Amazon jungle. We've got to act quickly.''

Beeker nodded. "We can be ready inside of a week. I think it would be best if we went in separately, using civilian transport and bogus identities, since they seem to know what we're up to. Where are we supposed to meet Guiterrez?''

"His men will pick us up outside of Cusco,'' Jackie replied, referring to the ancient mountain capital of the

Incas, nestled deep in the country's south-central Andean highlands. "They'll bring us to him from there, but it's up to us to find the rendezvous point ourselves."

"That shouldn't be a problem," Beeker assured her. "We can all meet in Lima in one week's time, hitch on to a tourist-group flight to Cusco, and arrange transport into the hills from there. We can handle all the details—all you have to worry about is getting yourself to Lima with an intact cover identity. Your boss should be able to do that easily enough, much easier than he'll be able to dispose of those bodies in there." He motioned with his head toward the bathroom. Jackie's jaw dropped when she realized what he meant.

"What? How the hell do you expect us to get rid of those bodies without arousing suspicion? You can't saddle us with that responsibility!"

Beeker laughed with his mouth. "Not my problem," he said without a trace of hesitation. "Those characters turned up before I agreed to take this job, so they're yours to deal with. Starting now, any problem of a similar nature is mine to solve." He stood up and brushed off his clothes. "Any further negotiation can go through Maggie. She has full authority to act as my agent in this matter. Payment should be made through her. Otherwise, I'll see you in Peru in one week's time."

He turned, gave Maggie a short wink, and left the room.

# 4

The Black Berets were waiting for him when he got back to the farm the next afternoon. He had had Tsali use his computer to send messages for all of them to be there—sober and ready to work—the evening after his cold meat luncheon with Jackie and Maggie. Still, he was surprised to find them sitting in the farmhouse, energetic and clear-eyed, eager to hear the details of his trip to New York. He barely opened the door before their shouts greeted him.

"What's the scoop, Sarge?" Rosie Boone was the first to manage a coherent sentence. He was sitting at one end of the living room couch, lean torso forward and arms resting on his knees, flipping through an issue of *Guns and Ammo*. Beeker dropped his bag just inside the door and surveyed the men around the room.

Harry Pappathanassiou's bulky six-foot-two inch frame filled the doorway leading to the kitchen. Obviously fresh from a swim in the lake, he was dressed in a khaki sweat suit with a white towel draped burnoose-style over his curly black hair. With his left hand he was dumping a large bottle of mineral water down his throat, and though his head was tilted back, his sharp green eyes never left Beeker's face. Billy nodded his greeting. From the kitchen he could hear short, quick chopping noises, instantly recognizable to him as a razor blade on glass. He didn't need to wonder what that was about.

"Cowboy," he called out. "That's the last I want to see of that shit until what we've got to discuss is decided upon. If we go to work, I don't want to see it until we get back. Understood?"

Sherwood Hatcher—Cowboy—came out of the kitchen with a guilty grin on his freckled face, sniffling heavily.

"Shoot, Billy, I just needed a little something to roust the bats from my head. A few weeks of married life and my brains turn to slush. A quick jolt only helps keep my mind on business." He scratched his nose compulsively.

Cowboy's cocaine habit was a matter of some concern to Beeker, as was any use of a possibly dangerous substance by his men. Though he kept his own drinking and drug intake to near nonexistent levels, Beeker wasn't foolish enough to try to prohibit any use by his men. Everyone had occasional need of a crutch or a release, and he didn't feel it was up to him to judge what his men chose as theirs. It only became his concern when it interfered with their work. Lives depended on the optimum functioning of every member of the Black Berets, and if Beeker thought that anything any of them was doing put that functioning in jeopardy, it was time for him to step in. So far he hadn't had to.

"C'mon, Beek, don't give us the silent Injun routine," Applebaum called from the living room floor. "We want to know what went down in New York." As always, Marty looked like he had just been roused from a sound sleep. His wispy brown hair stuck out from his head, his black-rimmed glasses sat crookedly on his prominent nose, and his clothes hung limply on his wiry frame. He had spread himself out on a plastic groundcloth in the middle of the living room floor, enthusiastically field-stripping his cut-down M-60.

"Relax, Applebaum. I'll get to it. First, I want you to finish scrubbing down your cannon."

39

"Yeah, Marty," Cowboy chimed in. "And maybe you should clean yourself as often as you do that M-60."

"Eat shit and die, Cowboy," Applebaum shot back. "Maybe you should try keeping your nose as clean as I keep this barrel."

There was general laughter at this familiar not-kidding/not-serious exchange. Beeker took a seat on the opposite end of the couch from Rosie and watched Applebaum assemble the greased metal pieces of his weapon. There was something fascinating in the way Marty handled the finely machined, lovingly lubricated parts of his M-60. It reminded Beeker of a cross between a kid's ecstatic enthusiasm for his first set of electric trains, a surgeon's confident ease with his tools, and a jazz saxophonist's physical lovemaking with his instrument.

Applebaum displayed a peculiar reverence for the cumbersome machine gun—all twenty-three and a half pounds of it. He'd been lugging the thing around with him ever since Nam, where he first picked it up because it looked big and mean—two qualities distinctly lacking in Applebaum's appearance. Since then, it had become like another limb of his body. He refused to go anywhere without it and hated fighting with any other weapon. He was more faithful to that M-60 than most men were to their wives. "No woman ever killed anything for me after I pulled *her* trigger," he liked to say. Applebaum loved saying ludicrous things like that. It came from watching too many old war movies.

"As soon as Mr. Firepower over here gets through putting his death machine back in its toy chest, we'll get down to business. We've got some decisions to make for ourselves."

Beeker's words had a tangible effect on the atmosphere in the room. Except for the boy, Tsali—who remained absorbed in the bright symbols parading across the

40

computer's screen display—the four men in the room looked at him with an intense seriousness. It was a look commonly found in groups of professionals when they're challenged to address the principles of work they deeply love. It was a look of commitment with the promise of fulfillment.

"There's a very basic question that we've got to answer," Beeker began, looking directly into each of his men's eyes, one after another. "This is something I've been giving a lot of thought to since we got back from Africa. Probably you guys have, as well. It's a simple thing, really. Are we mercenaries? Are we just a bunch of hired guns, contract killers? Is that what we want to do?"

Rosie answered first. "Sarge, you say that word, *mercenary*, like it puts a bad taste in your mouth. What's wrong with doing that? It's what we do best, isn't it? We're professional soldiers, right? We gotta face that—we gotta forget trying to be civilians and just do what we're most comfortable doing. I'm shitty at being a civilian. We all are. Hasn't this last couple of months taught us something?"

"Yeah," Harry said in his soft voice. "It taught me that I missed all you guys, and that I missed working with you. That fucking bar I had in Chicago was the *worst*." He shook his head and laughed with a derisive snort.

"Damn straight," Rosie said with emphasis. "We *all* hated what we were doing. Shit, Beeker, when you walked through the door of the Newark Municipal Hospital Morgue"—he shook his head ruefully—"I thought you were the Angel of Heaven come to deliver me from eternal damnation. I was in the shit mouth-deep, man, and you walked in and gave me a way out. That was my *dignity* you gave back to me." Rosie's eyes drilled into Beeker's like knife points.

"Rosie's right, Beek," Cowboy put in. "He's speaking

for all of us. We've been the walking dead since we got back from the Nam; stumbling around, getting ourselves into shit we wouldn't want no part of if we'd been in our right minds. This is where we *belong*, Billy. All of us.'' Both Harry and Marty grunted and nodded their agreement.

Harry picked up the train of thought. "It's just like 1970 again, Sarge, when you came looking for us to put together the SOG team. It was like we were all floating around, useless, waiting for you to scoop us up. We were meant for that gig, and we're meant for this one. Nothing much else matters.'' He shrugged.

There was silence for upward of a minute as Beeker worked through what had been said. It was perfectly clear, really. There wasn't much call for debate. They'd said what he'd hoped they would, and their words echoed his feelings as well. They were meant to fight, pure and simple. Life was hollow and meaningless without that ultimate of challenges. Will I kill or be killed? Will I prevail? Am I the king of this fucking jungle, or aren't I? Beeker needed to live on the knife edge that cut the separation between a life you go through because you've got nothing better to do and the kind of life you grab by the balls and squeeze till it submits to your way of doing things. That was the edge Beeker wanted to keep sharpened, and he knew it was the same for his men.

"That's settled, then,'' he said, breaking the long silence. "I'm glad you all feel that way. I just wanted to hear it. There's one other thing, though, that needs clarification. We're going to be working for *ourselves* this time. There is no MAC/V in command of this war, and that means no pussy-ass, map-reading generals giving us orders; pompous bastards more interested in keeping their gold stars shiny and their records spotless than they are in the welfare of their men in the field. No more of that shit. And no more CIA country-club case officers, and no politicians selling our asses down the river. We're independents now, and that means we take *nobody's* orders, do *nobody's* latrine duty, and kiss *nobody's* hindquarters. We take only work that we *want* to take, for reasons we don't have to explain to *anybody*. We're in business for ourselves when the money's right and when we all agree that the setup suits us. We will *not* work for scum or thieves or murderers or anyone, just because they have the money to pay. We will not be bought. . . ."

Silence again followed. Applebaum broke it.

"Kinda like high-class hookers, eh, Sarge?" He giggled nervously and, when none of the others joined him, stopped abruptly. "All I meant was that we're choosy . . . that's all," he said lamely. "I mean, you know I'd follow you into anything, Sarge. I'm not much on decision-making and that sort of shit . . . that's why I need you. You just point me somewhere and say to me, 'Marty, that bridge needs blowing,' and I go do it. No problem. I don't like having to think about whether what I'm doing is right or not. That just gets things all confused. I don't want to have to worry about any of that stuff. I just want to do my job and enjoy it."

"The Runt's got a point, Sarge." Rosie said. "Being soldiers, we're a little uncomfortable with democracy. We appreciate your wanting to give us a voice in the decision-making, but Applebaum's right—we just want someone to point us in the direction of a job that needs doing. You're our decision-maker, Beek, and we all trust you more than we trust our mothers. We know that if you say something's okay for us to do, it's okay. We woulda followed you up Ho Chi Minh's left nostril in Nam, and that's still the case. You're our conscience, Beek, and we're gonna accept whatever you think is right."

"Yeah, and it was me that almost got us killed going back to Laos."

"C'mon, Beek, you aren't blaming yourself for that, are you? We all knew what kind of slime Parkes was. We all knew there had to be something going on besides what he was telling us. We were just too damn itchy to get back in action to stop and think. We would've bought *any* bullshit story handed to us, and you know it. We wanted back in so bad that we got sloppy, and so we got burned a little bit. But we burned 'em back more than enough to make up for it, didn't we? Ain't nobody blaming you for that one, Sarge."

"Nobody but me," Beeker said.

"Well, just forget it, Sarge. Ain't none of us gonna let you pin that rap on yourself. If there's any guilt to be served out, we all deserve equal shares."

"I don't know, Rosie. I understand what you're saying, and thanks, but after what happened, I just don't see how I can trust my own judgment."

Harry answered. "We're all trusting you, Sarge, and there's no one else in the world that we'd rather trust our lives to. You know all of our capabilities, Sarge, and you know your own. If *you* think we can do it and think we *should* do it, then that's good enough for us. Everything else is *skata me rigani!*" Harry reached into the bowels of his ancestry for the last phrase—it meant "shit with oregano." The Greeks certainly had a colorful way with vulgarity.

Beeker grinned. "Okay." He squirmed uncomfortably. "And thanks. Your faith in me means a lot. But you'll have to promise me that you'll keep me in line—kick my butt if I ever get out of hand; frag my ass if I ever lead you somewhere you don't want to go."

"No problem at all, Sarge," Rosie reassured him. "Leadership is based on respect. As soon we lose our respect for you, we'll just stuff Applebaum's asshole full of C-4 and drop him on your face while you sleep. That'd solve the problem!''

They laughed long and hard at that. Especially Applebaum, and his hysterical whooping cackle made the others laugh even harder. The warmth between them grew to the point where you could practically feel the temperature of the room rising. The bond between them—one of the strongest of bonds uniting men, that of comrades in battle—grew as well. Their brotherhood had stood the test, and Beeker felt closer to them than he had ever felt to any other human beings. The Black Berets were more than just his family. They were his very life.

Their laughter quieted after a few minutes but continued long enough to rouse Tsali from his computer reverie. He came over to Beeker with inquisitiveness in his bright, boy's eyes, and sat on the floor at his adopted father's feet. Rustling the boy's hair with his right hand, Beeker felt happy and ridiculous at the same time. It was like a scene out of *Leave It to Beaver*—domestic bliss—and while it felt good, it also was difficult for him to feel comfortable with it. Maybe if his childhood had been happier, this wouldn't have confused him quite so much. Maybe if he'd known his father. . . .

''Okay,'' he said, feeling a bit like a scoutmaster calling his troop to order. ''Now that we're all loosened up and agreed on everything, let's talk about the business at hand. What I've got here is a relatively simple-sounding job that I'm more than a bit suspicious about. The money's good, and the people we're working for shouldn't be a problem. It's basically a baby-sitting run, but I'd be damn willing to bet that it turns out to be a lot more complicated than that. That's why we've got to cover as many of the angles as we can and make sure no one gets one over on us.''

Beeker then backed up in time and started telling them the story from the beginning. He told them about the letter

45

from Maggie O'Hare, and about their encounter in a basement stairwell of a New York office building. Then he told them about the hotel room conference with Maggie and Jackie Simmons and the two guys who did such a bang-up job serving lunch. He related the details of the job as outlined by Simmons and ended with his understanding of the situation and the first ideas of the plan he was starting to formulate.

"We'll get a hundred thousand for this job—with Maggie's commission added on top of that. After equipment costs, we should clear a good fifteen to seventeen thousand each. That's if everything goes without a hitch, which of course, we all hope it will. Of course, it won't. This guy Guiterrez seems to think we have no need of any weapons, but he's got another thing coming if he thinks we're gonna drop ourselves in unarmed. Cowboy, it'll be up to you to go to Colombia and arrange for some weapons and transport for them to an air drop in Peru, where we'll be waiting for you. You and I will work out the details later with a map."

Cowboy nodded. "With ten or fifteen thousand gringo dollars, I can buy *anything* in Colombia."

"Fine, but let's restrict it to instruments of an offensive and defensive nature, okay?"

Cowboy grinned his wide Texas grin. "No problem, Chief. What sort of tools do you think we'll need?"

Beeker paused thoughtfully. "We'll be traveling in both highland and jungle territory, and I think we should be prepared for the eventuality of field survival and leaving the country on our own."

"Like if something happens to Guiterrez and his men?" Rosie asked.

"Whatever," Beeker replied with a sweep of his hand. "From the possibility that government troops wipe them all out before we get there, to the possibility of a complete double-cross. I just don't trust guerrilla revolutionary leaders—they're too damn eager to sacrifice other people for their cause or their egos. I say we keep a few steps ahead of Mr. Guiterrez."

"Good thinking," Cowboy agreed. "I'll line us up some M-16s—you don't want to be carrying anything heavy in the heat. Plus, I'll pick up some jungle gear and freeze-dried rations in case you have to hoof it out. If you want them, I should be able to pick up a couple of heavy pieces—like an RPG-7, a LAW, or some M-203 grenade launchers. That do it for you?"

"You'll also be dropping us in some videotaping equipment, so we can record Jackie's interview. Can you pick up that sort of stuff down there as well?"

"Not as easy as guns but almost. All these coke tycoons love to buy expensive toys with their ill-gotten gains, so I should be able to scare us up a Hitachi mini-cam or Sony at the least."

"The rest of us will be flying down separately on civilian aircraft, with wet paper." Beeker used the old CIA field expression for forged documentation. "Rosie, Harry, and I will go in as surfers coming down from California—this is prime surf season in Peru, and they get thousands of beach bums down there looking for the perfect wave. Applebaum, since you're too scrawny to pass for a surfer on the best day of your life, you'll carry journalistic credentials—"

"Yeah, like *Sports Illustrated* swimsuit editor, huh?" Applebaum cut in.

"Yeah, something like that. We'll check in separately to the same hotel and meet in my room at ten o'clock that night for instructions. Today is Tuesday, right? We should all be in Lima by Sunday, ready to meet Jackie and fly to Cusco on Monday morning. Cowboy's drop will be scheduled for Tuesday afternoon, and the rendezvous with

Guiterrez's men for sometime the next day. I want us out of the country by the weekend at the latest, with Cowboy standing by with transportation in case we need it. I don't trust Guiterrez to get us out of there intact. It might fall back on us to handle that. And judging by the way our luck's been running, it probably will.

"That just about covers it, I think. Any questions?" He looked around at the faces of his men, searching for uncertainty. Too often people will ask themselves a question they should be asking aloud.

"What happens if we get picked up by the locals?" Rosie asked. "I don't think they'll take too kindly to men with guns wandering around their country. What's to prevent them from burying us somewhere?"

Beeker nodded. "Good point. That's where working for Maggie comes in handy—she's got insurance that covers bail-out money, and powerful friends to look after us. And, as a last resort, there are other people like us who'll get us out if asked to."

Rosie grinned. "That's reassuring. I suppose we can trust her, right?"

"I think so," Beeker answered truthfully. "In the first place, her pedigree is impeccable. And I liked the way she handled herself in that hotel room—that's what clinched it." He laughed and shook his head at the memory. "You guys should've seen her, tearing the shit out of that guy's ear."

"Yeah," Applebaum added, "and that's not the only part of a man's body she can take off with her teeth. I ain't so sure hooking up with her is a good idea. . . ."

"What's your problem, Runt? I thought you were fond of the girl.. Why, you even told me—"

Applebaum interrupted, eyes darting nervously. "Yeah, well, that was a long time ago. I don't even remember too well what happened . . . we'd been drinking a little bit . . ."

Rosie's lips parted in an evil grin, like a hungry predator about to pounce on its helpless prey. "Well, Marty, tell us more. I don't believe we've heard about this one before. God knows you've told us about all the rest. I guess there's just been so many of the little darlings that this one just got forgotten, eh? C'mon, Marty—is she or isn't she a real redhead?"

Applebaum squirmed uncomfortably on the floor, nervously poking at his assembled M-60 with distracted ineffectiveness, his squirrelly eyes averting everyone else's. Harry stepped in to the rescue, as he usually did when Marty got himself in trouble.

"Ease off, Rosie," he said quietly. The black man shot him a resentful glare.

"Well, maybe the little worm ought to think a little before he shoots his mouth off. That just might save you the trouble of sheepdogging his candy-coated butt all the time."

Beeker broke in. "Can it, you two." As always, response to their leader's words was instantaneous. Both Boone and Applebaum wiped their faces clean of expression and patiently awaited his next words. It was the sort of disciplined obedience Beeker demanded—and got—from his men. When the change of atmosphere was fixed in the air, Beeker continued.

"I think taking jobs steered our way through Maggie is a good idea. First of all, we get to pick and choose. Nothing is written anywhere that says we have to *take* everything she points us to. She's not our boss, just our agent. And as one of the best-known and best-repped agents in the business, she'll be getting us only class work—work that we want. That means no jobs showing Iranian teenagers how to strangle old women. We'll get

49

the best, most challenging work the world has to offer, and get paid top dollar for it. Maggie knows us, both from her own research and from what I've told her, and she knows what kind of work we can do. I think it'll turn out to be a good arrangement all around.''

This time there was no disagreement.

"Good. As of now, we are on full action status. That means no drugs or alcohol, regular sleeping and eating schedules, and complete daily workouts. Each of us will give Cowboy a list of the equipment we think we'll need in-country. Make sure it includes nothing you might regret carrying on your back. Rosie, I want you to make the travel arrangements. Spread us over as many flights—'' Beeker was interrupted by a tug on his right pant leg. It was Tsali, motioning to himself, and then at the computer, with a broad smile on his face.

"Tsali's got this great new toy,'' Cowboy offered, by way of translation. "Hooks the computer up to the phone so's it can call other computers and do things to 'em. I bet he can put us on the plane right through that little keyboard there.'' Tsali's head was bouncing up and down vigorously.

Beeker laughed and rubbed the boy's hair again. "Okay, Tsali, you can be our travel agent. Just be sure our connecting flights are in the right sequence.''

Eagerly, Tsali hopped up off the floor and ran to the table in the corner of the living room where the computer terminal sat. It was his chance to contribute something unique to the work of the Black Berets, and he grabbed for it. Tsali was carving out a niche for himself, a position on the team for him and him alone to play. He was not content to follow in anyone's footsteps; he wanted to plant his own in the ground. Again, Beeker was proud.

"That should be it, then,'' he said, and glanced at his watch. "Lights out will be at midnight, reveille at eight sharp, and a morning jog down by the lake at eight-twenty.''

Applebaum groaned. "Shit, it's G.I. Joe time again. And I was just starting to get loosened up."

"C'mon there, Runt. A little trot never hurt anyone, not even a faggot weasel like you," Cowboy said, laughing.

Beeker left them to their good-natured ribbing and took his overnight bag to his room. It was amazing what the promise of action at a specified time in the near future did for a group of fighting men. They had become both relaxed and energized, confident and pleasantly apprehensive—something like a man who had suddenly realized he was going to get laid that night. Petty bickering was forgotten. Tensions evaporated. Reasons for arguments were instantly unremembered. Comradeship was restored undamaged. Beeker wished it could always be like this—the adrenaline rush of imminent action transformed into a permanent high. It was a bit too much to expect, though.

After unpacking his bags and putting his body through some tension-relieving calisthenics, Beeker still felt too restless to sleep. Doubts gnawed at his stomach; uncertainty eroded the rock of his Marine self-confidence. He decided to go for a walk in the woods and let the thoughts tear-assing through his head run themselves out of steam. He knew he'd never get to sleep if he didn't.

Outside it was a brisk winter night; the sky was cloudless and star-filled, and a near-full moon hung low in the south. He walked past the garage where Cowboy's small Beechcraft was stowed and continued leisurely through the down-sloping clearing toward the lake. The night was silent except for his breathing, his footfalls in the ankle-high grass, and the occasional far-off howling of a chained-up, lonesome hound. A single nagging thought kept repeating itself inside his head: *Am I doing the right thing?*

It wasn't just a simple matter of taking on a job or not; it was more than that. Saying yes to this job meant saying yes to a whole new life. It would mean turning his back for good on a quiet, normal, civilian existence—giving up any hope he might have had left that he could forsake the warrior's life and become what was considered a "useful member of society." He knew he was ill-suited for that life, but at the same time he felt like he couldn't just walk away from it. It would be like leaving a house you've lived in for a while—however unhappily—and forever closing the door behind you. Could he do it?

And there was more. As much as Billy Leaps Beeker prided himself on his independence, he had always been a good Marine. A good Marine *sergeant*. That meant following the orders and planning of other men. When he was an eighteen-year-old jarhead-in-training at Parris Island—ink still fresh on his sign-up papers—he thought those orders came from men smarter and more able to make the right decisions than he. When he left the Corps in disgust almost ten years later, he was convinced otherwise. Now that he was in the business of making his own decisions, he felt the heavy responsibility of that position—the precariousness of it and the fear of looking down into the bottomless drop of failure. There was little comfort for the man who had to lead his men into that well of darkness. Was he up for it? These doubts had never troubled him in Vietnam, leading his men almost daily into death's bloody grip. But this was different; the looming bulk of the U.S. Marine Corps was no longer behind him. The Black Berets were on their own.

The faint sensation of a movement behind him brought Beeker out of his thoughts and into readiness. Rosie Boone drifted like a shadow out of the night.

"Taking a stroll, Billy?" He asked casually.

"Yeah. I guess I'm not so sure about all this. Thought some night air might help straighten me out."

"Well, if that don't, *this* sure will. Delilah's on the

52

phone, and she's pulling the Ice Queen routine. You want to talk to her?''

Beeker thought about that. He knew what she was going to say. Did he want to hear it?

Back inside, he picked up the phone from the table and put it to his ear.

"Yeah?" He said in his best D.I. growl.

"I *asked* you not to take this job, Billy. Now I'm *telling* you. Drop it, *now*, before it's too late. This is a hot one. You have no idea what you're getting yourself into." This time her voice wasn't soft and seductive; it had a knife edge you could skin a deer with. And it was nearby.

"Is that a threat?"

"No, you hardheaded jerk-off, it's a *warning*. This job will be hazardous to your health, do you hear me? It isn't cowboys and Indians we're talking about. This is heavy people with lots of money and power. You're getting in over your head. Leave it alone."

Beeker said nothing and allowed Delilah's words to rattle around in his head for a bit. When the words butted up against the rigid wall of his anger, he reacted.

"Are you through?" he asked her tonelessly.

"I think I've made my point," her voice came back. "If you're still too dense to hear it, then that's not my problem."

Beeker smiled. "You know, Delilah, you've got a real gift. There's something in the way you tell me to do something that immediately makes me want to do the opposite. I've had my doubts about this thing a couple of times—but after talking to you, I make up my mind *real* fast. Thanks for the help."

"Billy—"

Beeker hung up on her again. He knew then that he would have no trouble sleeping that night.

53

# 5

Beeker's sixth-floor room in the Hotel Simón Bolívar over-
looked Lima's busy Plaza San Martín and, beyond that, to
the northwestern edge of Peru's sprawling capital city.
Except for the rapidly redeveloping downtown area—
clustered between Beeker's hotel and the city's main square,
the Plaza de Armas—Lima was essentially a low-rise city.
Two- and three-story adobe brick residences spread crazy-
quilt past the city's original northern boundary—the Rímac
River—and as far westward toward the dim Andean foot-
hills as the eye could see.

It was sorta like a primitive L.A., Beeker thought, only
without the car-bound mega-distances and stubbornly sub-
urban atmosphere that made L.A. such an awful place.
Here it was, nearly ten o'clock in the evening on Beeker's
watch, and people were still walking the streets. *Nobody*
walked in L.A. Ever. Admittedly, this was the height of
the "carnival" tourist season, but there was something
about Lima that told Beeker people probably walked here
all year round. Strolling human figures certainly made an
urban environment more pleasant. Even more pleasing to
Beeker's rural eye was the city's conspicuously thriving
rooftop culture. Nearly every house in the city utilized its
roof area for either family gatherings, gardening, or storage space, thanks to an almost rain-free climate. It really
dressed up the normally bleak view of a city's rooftops,

which always looked to Beeker like something you were never supposed to see—like the false backdrop of a Hollywood set. And it was only fitting that Lima, of all cities, should have such an excitingly chaotic hairline, considering its Indian inhabitants' obvious obsession with hats.

A knock at the door brought Beeker back. He pulled the wall-sized curtains shut and crossed the room—which he'd noted as far bigger than his ten-times more expensive one in New York—to admit a smiling Roosevelt Boone.

"*Que pasa*, Sarge?" He asked, breezing into the room.

"*Nada, amigo,*" Beeker responded. "Any entry problems?"

He shook his head. "Nope, not a one. They gobbled the 'Adam Break, Surfin' Spade' routine right up. Told them I was headed nonstop for the beach at Miraflores, and they were all smiles. They took the entry half of my tourist card, bowed politely, and pointed me at the water." He sat down and stretched himself out luxuriously. "Y'know, I think I like this guy—maybe I'll use old Adam again someday." He laughed with self-congratulatory pleasure.

"Hey," Beeker cautioned him, "let's worry about this gig first—like whether we'll get out of here without any new cracks in our asses—before we start planning future impersonations, okay?"

"You bet, Bwana Sarge," Boone drawled with exaggerated disrespect, throwing Beeker a pathetic salute. Just then, another knock at the door sounded. Beeker admitted Applebaum and Harry the Greek, completing the male contingent of the expeditionary force. Only Jackie Simmons remained unaccounted for.

"Any problems to report so far?" Beeker asked his two men. Both indicated negative—Harry with a characteristically understated nod of his head, and Applebaum with loud proclamations of his prowess at selling border officials any line of bullshit he pleased.

55

"You shoulda seen me, Beek. I was magnificent," he concluded. He waved his pale, bony arms theatrically around his head, causing the gaudy Hawaiian shirt he was wearing to flap against his ribs. Ducking into the bathroom, he helped himself to a bottle of Inca-Kola from the stocked ice bucket next to the sink. Harry poured himself a cup of the strong local coffee. Even though the night air was rather mild—in the mid-sixties—the humidity was quite high, and the muscular Greek had already soaked his cotton T-shirt through with sweat. In Vietnam, he'd had to drink constantly in order to keep from becoming dehydrated. Salt tablets were also a dietary staple in those years. He was obviously uncomfortable but, typically, didn't complain.

"We'll wait till Jackie gets here before going over most of what I want to say," Beeker began. "But there's a few things I want to make clear before she arrives. This whole setup gives me the creeps, so I want you guys on your toes for the entire time we're here. We're naked here. We got no backup; both sides of this little war may start shooting at us and we're carrying wet paper. Everything might seem fine now, but let the locals get one whiff of what we're *really* up to, and we've had it. So I can't emphasize this enough—be careful! Break absolutely no laws that you don't have to, and attract as little attention to yourselves as possible. And we'll have to nursemaid Jackie more than we'd like, I'm sure. You'll see what I mean when she gets here. But she's the weak link on this team and we're gonna have to hold up her end if we're gonna make it. We have to protect her, but we've got to protect ourselves as well. Completing the job comes first—that means getting Jackie and her story out of here—but let's not get wasted for some TV network's scoop. We've got to use our brains and do things the smart way and the safe way."

A light knock prevented Beeker from continuing his lecture. "That'll be Jackie," he said hopefully. It was.

Her appearance made Beeker want to puke. She had on a wide-brimmed straw hat, circled with a bright red ribbon that trailed down her back. Her eyes were covered with large, red-framed plastic sunglasses, and her lips were waxed to a glossy sheen. Cream-white baggy pants flowed around her legs, and her gauzy cotton blouse was belted tightly with a red silk scarf. Earrings tinkled like wind chimes, and dark brown nipples winked hello as she sashayed into the room. Her effect on the room was instantaneous, as she must've known it would be. It was as though the first hooker of the day had entered a dockside bar full of sailors who hadn't seen a woman in months. Beeker cursed to himself. This job was going to be even worse than he'd imagined.

"Jackie," he began, hoping that if he ignored her carefully landscaped appearance everyone else would, too. "This is Roosevelt Boone, Marty Applebaum, and Harry Pappathanassiou. We'll all be with you from now on. Have a seat, and we'll get under way." The men nodded at her, a bit awestruck, while she merely smiled seductively, as if secretly enjoying her obvious power over them. Beeker had always despised women like her; women who exploited their biological power over men almost indiscriminately, for the sheer pleasure of domination that it gave them.

"Beeker, you redskinned savage," Marty said, his voice obnoxiously suave. "Offer the lady a drink. Don't you have any manners?" He grinned stupidly at her while Beeker drilled him with an ugly look.

"Oh, a Coke would be just fine," she said with a laugh. "I don't want you to go to any trouble for me."

Right, Beeker thought. No trouble at all, honey. Probably get us all killed and not even notice it. His stomach performed a silent war dance inside him. Outside, only a slowly clenching fist betrayed his anger. After Marty had finished pouring her a glass of Coke—staring at her chest throughout—Beeker began his talk. The sound of his own voice, firm and steady, and the thought of business calmed him.

"We're all booked on the nine thirty-five AeroPerú flight tomorrow morning from Jorge Chavez Airport. We'll all check in separately, arriving in different taxis. When we get to Cusco, we'll again travel separately to our hotel. We all have rooms waiting for us at the Hotel Espinar, which is a good three-star place in the center of town. We've got to spend the rest of Monday taking it easy— Cusco is more than two miles high, and if you don't give your body a chance to adjust, it'll just give out on you. The locals call the condition *soroche*, but basically it's good old oxygen deprivation. If you feel shortness of breath, headache, heart palpitations, giddiness, and—at its worst— vomiting, lie down right away. Rosie has some coramina glucosa, which should help with the symptoms, but basically all you can do is rest until your body catches up with things. And most important—no alcohol whatsoever. That just makes everything worse."

"I understand men also lose their fertility for a week at high altitudes. Is that true, Billy?" Jackie asked demurely.

Beeker muttered "Christ" under his breath and rolled his eyes. Rosie answered for him.

"That's right, darlin'. But just you remember, it's only the ability to impregnate we lose, not the ability to try. And just in case you want to test—"

"That'll do, Boone," Beeker broke in. From Applebaum he expected this sort of garbage, but Rosie? He hadn't bargained on playing chaperon for a bunch of horny hounds and a bitch in heat. Things grew worse with every passing

58

minute. He resumed his briefing as a way of restoring order.

"Cowboy's due to drop our supplies on Tuesday evening. We've picked a good spot nearby on the map—about twenty kilometers due north on a relatively uninhabited, open plateau. We'll reconnoiter the drop zone that afternoon, so it won't be too much of a surprise in the dark. We can't use any flares or bright lights, so I've arranged something with Cowboy using an infrared signaling device I brought in as some of my camera equipment. We've got to effect the drop, recover the equipment, and evacuate the DZ as quickly as we can. I don't want us attracting any attention, and I don't want us around if anyone comes looking. We'll get as far away as we can, make camp for the night, and set out north the next morning for our rendezvous with Guiterrez's men.

"When they meet us and start taking us into the mountains, I want all of you to remember as much of the route as you can. Take note of any landmarks on the trail that you notice, and keep yourself oriented with the highest mountain peak you can see. I understand there are two particularly striking ones in the area. I'll be doing a bit of surreptitious blazing on the trail myself, and I don't want any of you duplicating that and increasing the chances of our guides noticing. Give all appearances of trusting them completely, but never turn your backs on any of them. Keep your weapons concealed until I order otherwise. I don't want them knowing we've got insurance. Let that be a surprise when the time comes—it might just save our asses."

"Billy, I still think you're going through an awful lot of trouble for nothing," Jackie said. "I don't see why you don't trust Guiterrez and his men. We're here to help them, aren't we? Why should they want to be anything less than honest with us?"

"Because this ain't Disneyland, and I just don't trust them. Just let me worry about that. It makes me feel better if I'm prepared for the worst. If it's all for nothing, we'll get a good laugh about it later. If not, you'll thank me if we make it out alive. Fair enough?"

Jackie shrugged indulgently. It was like she was saying, "Oh, go ahead and play your little game, you silly man, if it makes you feel so important. I'll humor you, but I know what a pathetic charade it is." Beeker's fist went to work again. He hoped he'd make it through this job without breaking Jackie Simmons's cute little jaw. At the moment it was calling out to him, "Punch me, punch me!" He ignored the invitation.

"Just one more thing before we call it a night. I hope you brought some other clothes, Jackie. Because what you're wearing certainly wouldn't make it where we're going. The terrain up there is damn rugged—we'll be going from both dense jungle to mountainous highlands, from ninety-degree days to thirty-degree nights. On top of that, it's the rainy season, which means we get dumped on every afternoon for a few hours. We're not going on a catered day trip to the country here; it'll be one rough bit of traveling. Do you understand that?"

Jackie waved a delicate hand in his direction. "Of course, I'm aware of that, Sergeant Beeker. Will you please stop treating me like a Girl Scout on her first trip to summer camp. I'm not a novice at this; I've done my homework. I've covered war zones, for God's sake, so don't go on at me as though I don't know what I'm doing. Men like you always think women can't take care of themselves—and that we can't wait for some big strong brute to come riding in on his white horse and save us from everything. There *are* some women in the world who can take damn good care of themselves. We don't all faint dead away when the going gets tough. I might not be able to shoot a man in cold blood, but I can handle myself quite nicely when it counts."

In the interest of group harmony, Beeker refrained from arguing. Applebaum made it harder by laughing like a kid who's just seen his friend get scolded by the teacher.

"Atta girl, Jackie," he cheered. "Some men just don't know how to deal with a real woman!" The idiotic leer on Applebaum's bony face was obviously meant to indicate that he, on the other hand, knew damn well how to deal with real women. Beeker sighed silently and felt his stomach take a turn for the worse.

The flight the next morning went without a hitch. It was a ninety-minute hop over the mountains to Cusco's Quispiquilla Airport, and Beeker enjoyed every minute of it. From his window seat on the half-empty 727—the highlands are an unpopular vacation spot during the rainy season—Beeker watched some of the most beautiful mountain scenery he'd ever laid eyes on. The Andes ran through the center of Peru like a double-columned spine, separating the scrubby, near-desert coastline (a lot like California, Beeker thought) from the thick, triple-canopied Amazon rain-forest (a lot like Vietnam, Beeker thought). The mountains rose quickly out of the low, brownish-green carpet that hugged the coastline, piercing the ever-present cloud cover with spectacularly jagged stone fingers. Once through the ceiling of puffy white mist, the plane skirted its way through a forest of snow-covered peaks. The clouds dissipated over the central plateau, revealing miles of rolling green grasslands that before long gave way again to sky-reaching mountains. Beeker was almost sorry when the heavily forested slopes of the Cordillera Vilcabamba— the final mountain retreat of the ravaged Inca empire four and a half centuries ago, and now staging ground for

Ramon Guiterrez's revolutionary army—rolled into view, signaling their imminent arrival in Cusco.

Beeker's room in the Hotel Espinar wasn't quite as big or comfortable as the one in Lima, but it was fine. He didn't immediately notice the lack of oxygen as he'd expected—how can you sense something's thinner when you can't feel it in the first place?—but after carrying his bag from the baggage area to a taxi, and then up to his room at the hotel, he did notice a distinct lack of energy. Better stretch out and take it easy for a while, he decided, before wandering out in search of lunch. He swung open the room's wide windows to admit some of the cool mountain air, and lay down on the bed. The steady rotation of the ceiling fan soon hypnotized him into a shallow sleep.

Close to two hours later he rolled off the bed, changed his shirt, splashed some cold water on his face, and headed out. On the desk clerk's advice, he decided on a restaurant called El Retabillo, better known to its patrons as John's Bar, a favorite hangout of Cusco's American expatriate community. A good place to blend in anonymously, Beeker figured. As good a place as you can find four thousand miles from home. But first he wanted to stroll the city's narrow cobblestoned streets to acclimate himself a bit more to the alien atmosphere.

Although almost no physical evidence of it remained, Cusco had once been the fabulously gold-encrusted capital of a vast, thriving empire. The city had ruled over a domain that stretched thousands of miles north and south along the Andean ridge. Commonly called the Incas, they really had no name for themselves, as they weren't so much a people as a multitribal business organization. The Inca was their Chairman of the Board, overseeing the efficient operation of this tightly controlled conglomerate from the safe haven of his mountaintop fortress.

Like Rome a thousand years earlier, all roads led to Cusco. This two-mile-high city—village, really—nestled in a river valley on the shoulders of the Andes, formed the hub of the empire's skeletal and circulatory systems: the brilliantly engineered network of roads that wound through jungle and mountain terrain, uniting the tribute-hungry Inca with the most distant outpost of his domain. In the ancient Qechua language, Cusco meant ''navel of the earth,'' and according to legend it was founded on the spot where Manco Capac—the first Inca—touched his golden staff to the earth and watched the fertile ground swallow it completely. By Manco's decree, the city was modeled on the silhouette of a puma, the symbol of power and nobility.

Beeker climbed to the puma's head, the city's defending fortress of Sacsayhuaman, to survey the area from high ground. It was from here in 1533 that Francisco Pizarro's men pried gold plates off the walls to collect their ransom for the captured Inca. Three years later it was the launching point for Manco II's final siege on the captured capital; a siege that succeeded only in burning off every thatched roof in the valley. From there, Manco II retreated north into the forbidding Vilcabamba range, where he would hold out for forty years, futilely harassing the Spanish occupying forces.

Though nothing but huge foundation stones were left for Beeker to see, he could still tell that the fort had been one hell of an engineering feat, and an incredible fortress. He stood at the top of one of the crumbling, terraced walls and looked south over the crowded jumble of red-clay shingled roofs and tall, adobe-mud church towers. The puma's torso in the design had been defined by two now-invisible rivers—the Tullumayo and the Huantanay—which ran through wide stone culverts at street level, carrying the

63

city's waste down into the larger Vilcanota River. Sweeping the points of the compass from east to west—Beeker's left to right—his eyes took in first a scaled-down version of the landmark statue of Christ the Redeemer that stands over Rio de Janeiro and the jagged, snow-covered peak of Pachatusan—"Fulcrum of the Universe"—looming in the distance behind it. Opposite him were the words "Viva el Perú," inscribed on the side of a hill (ancient habits die hard, Beeker knew), and underneath that, the designation of the local army garrison, B-19. To his rear, amid the towering mountains that guarded the so-called "Sacred Valley of the Incas"—the lushly green, breathtakingly beautiful Urubamba River valley—lay the scrubby altiplano (high-altitude plateau) earmarked for Cowboy's equipment drop the following evening.

Standing up here, alone with the wind and sky, Beeker could feel something stir deep inside him. It was an instinctive response in his soul—the soul of a proud Cherokee warrior—to a spiritual presence that resided here. It was an intangible presence, like the air, but ancient and powerful, like the indomitable mountains that stood silent vigil over these reminders of lost grandeur. The Inca civilization itself might be gone, but its ghost haunted the land. Much as Beeker's ancient homeland had been obliterated by the white man, who'd raped it until it was unrecognizable to those who loved and respected it, the Spanish conquerors had wiped Cusco clean of native character. But no man, no matter how ruthless, could destroy forever the heritage of a land. It was still here, quiet perhaps, but Beeker's attuned senses could feel it. He breathed it deep into his lungs, and it felt good. Good men died here, maybe some still lived here.

His minutes of silent meditation continued, until gathering storm clouds in the east brought him back to the present. The rainy season's daily, late-afternoon shower was on its way, and he had no intention of getting caught up here when it came. While descending the steps back to town, his stomach growled. He was hungry.

He just managed to beat the rain to John's Bar. The place was pretty much what he'd expected: big, dark, and filled with noisily drinking gringos. He ordered *rocotos rellenos*—a local specialty of stuffed red peppers—from the smiling waitress, and it turned out to be quite good. He was finishing the last of the corn on the cob that came with it when something appearing in the door nearly made him choke. It was Jackie Simmons, with Applebaum on one arm and Rosie on the other. He had told them to keep an eye on Jackie but to avoid her company. So much for orders.

They were laughing loudly, but since everyone else in the joint was doing the same, they didn't seem to be attracting any undue attention. They didn't notice Beeker hugging the shadows in the rear, and took a highly visible table in the front of the dining room. They all ordered drinks, disregarding another of Beeker's specific instructions. His temper shifted into a slow burn. He had to break this little party up and *quick*.

Rising from his seat, he scooped up his cup of hot herbal tea and headed in their direction. He got as far as Rosie's back before he stumbled and dumped his tea over the black man's right shoulder.

Not surprisingly, Boone jumped. "What the fu—?" he shouted.

"Oh, I'm *so* sorry, sir!" Beeker said obsequiously. "How ridiculously clumsy of me! I hope I haven't ruined anything. Here, let me clean your shirt." Beeker reached for a napkin on the table, upending a Bloody Mary into Applebaum's lap.

"Oh, dear," he said. "I seem to have done it again! I

can't understand *why* I'm so clumsy. It must be this altitude. I guess I should have stayed in the hotel, like I was told." He put a bit of emphasis on the last phrase to get his message across. The three at the table just stared at him, dumbfounded.

"You *must* accompany me to my hotel, so I can repair some of the damage I've done here. Please, I insist!"

Boone's and Applebaum's astonishment was turning into annoyance. Jackie looked amused.

"I don't really think that'll be necessary," Boone was saying, blotting his scalded chest with a napkin.

"No, I really must *insist*!" Beeker repeated with emphasis. "It would be the only proper thing for me to do. I won't take no for an answer." He lifted both men by one armpit each. Then, turning to Jackie, he said, "But I don't see any reason why *your* lunch should be interrupted, ma'am. Why don't you just stay here and finish your meal while I try to make up for my clumsiness with these fine gentlemen. You *will* excuse us, I trust?" She smirked and nodded at Beeker as he escorted his men to the door.

Outside he flew into a rage. "I thought I told you assholes not to fraternize! You deliberately disobeyed my orders!"

Rosie shrugged sheepishly. Applebaum whined an explanation. "It was all the broad's idea, Beek. Honest! She called me up and did this heavy breathing number on the hotel phone, like she couldn't wait to get in my pants. And when I got downstairs, this horny buck here was trying to move in on my territory!"

"Your territory, my ass, Runt-hole! She called *me* up first—bitch knows the difference between an ofay eunuch and the real thing."

Beeker broke in. "Can't you two see past the ends of your cocks? Don't you know what that slimy little bitch is up to? She's jerking both of you off to satisfy her own

66

ego—she's manipulating the two of you into fighting over her, and she's enjoying it! She won't be happy until she's got *all* of us wrapped around her fucking little finger, drooling for a taste of what she's waving under our noses.''

Applebaum sneered and waved a disdainful hand. ''Hell, Beek, you're just jealous because the lady doesn't fancy you.'' Rosie said nothing, but Beeker could tell by the look in his eyes that he agreed.

''Well, I give up. Go ahead and think what you want about her, but that's the last of my orders I want disobeyed. Is that clear? I don't care if she's climbing all over you and putting hickies on every square inch of your balls—if I say ignore her, I want her *ignored*. We're guards, not gigolos. Got it?''

The two grunted affirmatively, but Beeker could tell their hearts weren't in it.

''Good. Now get the fuck back to your hotel rooms, and leave that snake with tits alone. Each of us has a job to do in the morning, and I want everything taken care of by noon. No screw-ups. Dismissed—and I don't want to see your ugly mugs again until tomorrow.''

The rest of the night passed quietly for Beeker. He resisted the temptation to run a bed check, to make sure everybody was where they belonged. At this point, he wasn't sure he wanted to know if anyone wasn't. He was tired and not much in the mood to play scoutmaster. Let those two shitbrains chase Jackie's tail if they wanted to—they just better be damn sure it didn't interfere with their job. Beeker hoped it wasn't too naive to think they wouldn't let it. Right.

He awoke early the next morning feeling much better. His body was adjusting quickly to the rarefied atmosphere, and that made him eager to get on with things. He hoped

the others were feeling as good as he. He had an inoffen-
sively bland breakfast in the hotel restaurant and then hit
the cobblestones to take care of his morning assignment—
procuring maps of the local terrain from the Tourist Office
and Museum of Antiquities, in the guise of an adventurous
tourist. Rosie's job was to secure adequate field provisions,
while Applebaum was to rent a couple of Land-Rovers.
Beeker had assigned Harry to shadow Jackie. Mostly it
was to make sure she stayed out of trouble, but not a little
of Beeker's motivation was his lack of trust in the woman.
He wanted no surprises.

The maps were easily obtained, and Beeker was back in
his room to stash them in his bag by eleven. He packed
what few of his possessions he'd left around the room and
then checked out of the hotel. Finding the empty Land-
Rover as arranged—in the deserted service alley behind
the hotel—he dropped his bag under a tarp and strolled
nonchalantly to the point a few kilometers north of town
where Rosie was to pick him up. The road was a thin
asphalt strip—barely wide enough to allow two trucks to
pass each other—which followed the winding path of the
old Empire road north, to the temples, farms, storehouses,
and hillside villages that dotted the area surrounding the
Sacred Valley. Most of the area's roads were laid over
five-hundred-year-old beds. It just would've been too damn
expensive to blaze entirely new trails through the jungle
and mountain ranges. As he walked to the rendezvous
spot, Beeker imagined he was a young native runner carrying a beltful of the knot-encoded ropes that served the
Empire's record-keeping needs. It was amazing, but the
Incas had had neither a written alphabet nor the wheel.
Hard to believe they could get so far without *either* of
them, let alone both.

The Land-Rover, with Rosie at the wheel, reached the
rendezvous point a minute and a half after the appointed

time. Beeker emerged from the brush where he'd been resting and got in next to him. In the rear storage compartment were two blue nylon backpacks stuffed with charqui—dried llama meat—and other field-type rations.

"Any problems to report?" Beeker asked after Rosie had upshifted and resumed cruising speed.

"Negative. Food was simple, and Marty left the Rover where he was supposed to. Everything's smooth as shit."

Beeker grunted and looked at his watch. Their next rendezvous was scheduled for just under an hour from now in a village about twenty-five kilometers up the road. There, in Chinchero, they would meet up with the other Land-Rover, carrying Marty, Harry, and Jackie Simmons. He settled back in his seat and enjoyed the beautiful scenery in silence.

Chinchero was little more than a backwater, a muddy town of less than ten thousand people, which served as marketplace for the local *nativo* farmers and livestock breeders. Otherwise, there was little reason to live there and even less reason to visit. Not surprisingly, they were the only out-of-towners in sight, quite conspicuous as they rolled slowly down the rutted streets toward the central plaza. Not being a market day, there were only a scattered handful of locals on the street, carrying bundles of various things on their backs or herding three or four scruffy llamas with sticks. At the center of the town's main square was a large, circular fountain which, before the marvel of plumbing, had served as the locals' water supply. But many still appeared to have need of it; there were dozens of youngsters about, toting buckets, plastic jugs, and a few animal-skin sacks. Of all the inhabitants, these kids showed the most interest in the two Land-Rovers that were now parked in the plaza opposite the old church. Of course, it wasn't the people in the vehicles that drew their attention but the vehicles themselves. Beeker hoped they wouldn't get too much in his way.

After Rosie shut off the engine, Beeker hopped out and strolled casually to the other Land-Rover. Harry was the only one in sight, leaning against the hood with his arms crossed. A group of kids, clad in baggy shorts and stretched-out Smurf T-shirts, stood about ten yards away, eyeing him fearfully. He made no move to encourage their friendliness. Beeker came up next to him and rested his foot on the front bumper.

"Where's the rest of our party?" he asked the unsmiling Greek.

"Went off for a stroll a couple of minutes ago, to see the sights, I guess," he answered. "I told 'em you wouldn't like it, but Marty told me to can it." He shrugged his big shoulders. "So I did."

"Well, you were right. I *don't* like it."

Harry didn't answer. Rosie had come up behind them during Harry's explanation.

"I'll go get 'em," he volunteered, and turned on his heel before Beeker could say anything. Beeker let him go.

"How did our girl spend her morning?" he asked Harry.

"Didn't do anything worth watching. Mostly wandered around the market and bought a few overpriced, tourist-shit kind of things. Didn't talk to anyone except about prices, didn't give anything to anyone except money, and didn't take anything from anyone except the crap she bought."

"Where is it?"

Harry motioned with his head to the rear of the Land-Rover.

"Wrapped in newspaper on the seat, and the hat next to it."

Beeker checked the hat, a brightly embroidered Indian-

70

style thing with long earflaps, and unwrapped the basketball-sized bundle. He fingered the four clay figures, obviously freshly made but tossed around a bit to lend an aged appearance, and then replaced them. He wasn't looking for anything in particular; just making sure nothing was going on behind his back. Shouts from across the square caught his attention.

"Just who the hell do you think you are, Boone?" It was Applebaum, and he was obviously disturbed.

"Keep your mouth plugged, Runt. I'm just making sure the lady here doesn't get your greasy fingerprints all over her," Boone shouted back. Jackie was between them, holding them apart. She seemed to be enjoying it.

"Maybe you should let the lady make her own decisions. She's perfectly capable of making up her own mind, and I don't think she wants any of your frigging help!"

"Boys, boys!" Jackie was saying, like a Den Mother about to reward her boisterous Cubs with sweets.

"Cut it out, assholes! I'm getting damn tired of telling you two to shut up!" Applebaum and Boone quieted down. Jackie only smirked. Beeker went on, "Okay, we've got work to do. Rosie, Marty, and I will drive ahead to reconnoiter the DZ. Harry, you take Jackie in the other Rover and set up a camp off the road about three kilometers north of here. That's where we'll stay the night after the drop. I want the Rover covered so it's invisible from the road, and the camp far enough into the brush so it can't be seen, either. Mark a tree on the east side of the road so we can find you when we come back. According to the map, we've got to drive up the road for four or five klicks, where we'll hit the footpath into the altiplano. The DZ is a couple of klicks off the road. Questions?"

There were none.

"Good. Let's get going."

The drop zone looked perfect, Beeker noted with relief. It was always a crapshoot when planning depended totally on maps of dubious accuracy. This time, though, everything looked fine. Beeker stood with Applebaum and Rosie in a clump of stumpy trees, looking across a few hundred yards of downward-sloping grassland. Just out of their sight, the ground dropped in a series of terraced steps to the densely jungled Vilcanota River valley. In the distance, the snow-covered peaks of the eastern range of the Andes poked at the ceiling of clouds. Mountains rose behind the three of them as well, much closer than those across the river. A few mountain animals—goats and llamas—were grazing leisurely on the plateau, but otherwise it seemed uninhabited. It was an ideal place for a drop—flat, open, and isolated. Cowboy would be flying in from the northeast, hugging the river valley to avoid local radar as much as he could. Beeker would position himself at the north end of the DZ and begin sweep-flashing his JVR 500 infrared signaling device. Cowboy would pick up the invisible signal with his viewer and drop the cargo as close to the light's ground point as he could. Boone and Applebaum would be deployed at seventy-five-yard intervals along Cowboy's flight path. Recovery should be accomplished within ten minutes, the chutes buried in ten more, and the three of them back on the footpath to the road in a maximum total time of thirty minutes. Sounds simple, Beeker thought. He hoped it would come off as simply as it sounded.

They had no trouble finding the camp Harry had set up. But considering the trouble that started immediately after their arrival, Beeker almost wished they hadn't found the place. It was downright sickening what a normally reasonable man's sex drive would push him to sometimes. Neither Applebaum nor Boone could keep away from Jackie. They were drawn to her like hungry tomcats to an aromatic garbage can. Their facial expressions traveled back and forth between the suspicious glares they shot each other, and the simpering smiles they aimed at Jackie. She was eating it all up. Rosie would offer her a cigarette from his pack. Marty's arm would instantly shoot in, bearing a flaming lighter. Marty would offer her a drink from his canteen. Rosie would instantly produce a cup for her to drink it out of. It went on like this for over an hour. Beeker tried to ignore them by attempting sleep but gave up in disgust. The inevitable fight brought him to his feet.

"You little worm-fucker!" Rosie had lost his temper first. He was leaping across the ten feet of ground that separated him and Applebaum, hands ready to grab the recoiling Runt's throat. It wasn't often that the big black man's temper snapped, but when it did, he wasn't responsible for his actions. On a tear, he had to be tied down, incapacitated, or knocked unconscious before he would stop.

Beeker's right shoulder hit Boone's ribcage hard. His momentum knocked Rosie's trajectory off enough to save Applebaum's throat—but not enough to keep Boone's body from crushing the puny white man. Marty howled and tried to scramble away. Rosie's powerful arms prevented him from getting far. Beeker encircled Boone's torso with his right arm and tried to pull him off his furiously squirming victim. But Rosie was enraged and there was no stopping him. His hands, wriggling like a batch of angry snakes, were just about to find their resting place around Applebaum's neck when Beeker felt himself lifted off the ground.

Harry had stepped in, once again, to save Applebaum

73

from certain death. He was lifting Rosie by his shirt collar and leather belt, holding both him and Beeker about three feet above the ground. Boone swam like a harness-yoked Olympic freestyler, yelling obscenities at both Applebaum and Harry. Beeker let go and dropped to the ground. Harry swung his unencumbered burden away and tossed him a few feet from the campsite. But this undignified interruption only made Boone angrier. His face was horribly contorted, eyeballs ready to pop from their sockets, teeth bared. He charged at Harry, who just stared at him without moving.

Beeker's shoulder again intervened. This time he knocked Rosie to his knees and followed through by driving the raging man's chin into the dirt. His firmly implanted knee-cap prevented Boone from rising, and his left arm circled Rosie's jaw. Boone's spine was arched like a bow, his only movement the heaving of his chest. Beeker held him that way for ten seconds before saying anything.

"*Calm down*, Rosie," he said through clenched teeth. "I'm not letting you go until you calm *down*."

It took a full minute for Boone's breathing to return to normal. He said nothing, but Beeker could tell by the relaxing of his muscles that he was indeed calming down. Finally, after his body felt slack in Beeker's grasp, he released him. Boone stared at the ground without moving for a pregnant moment, then got up quickly and shook himself clean.

"Rosie—" Beeker began in a conciliatory tone.

"Fuck you, Beeker," Boone answered without looking at him. "I owe you one—I owe *all* of you one." He brushed himself off and strode angrily from the camp.

Billy watched him go. It was the first time he'd ever had to turn on one of his men. He didn't like the feeling it left him with. Any leader that had to do that in order to keep discipline wasn't any kind of a leader. A wave of regret washed over him. He knew then that this whole job was a mistake. He hoped they'd make it out alive.

"I hope you're happy," he said tonelessly to Jackie, and walked away.

# 6

Unfortunately, Cowboy wasn't doing a hell of a lot better. Both the short hop to Miami and the direct flight from there to Bogotá went easily enough, though Cowboy was always a bit antsy when someone else was doing the flying. It occurred to him once that, very probably, the main reason he had taken up piloting was to get over his fear of flying. If he wasn't in direct control of the aircraft, then he was afraid. He made it his business after that to do as little commercial-flight flying as he could. Stick with his own wings and his own two hands. Except this time, Beeker had insisted on public transportation. Oh, well, he thought, a Valium and a few lines of coke should make it bearable—the former to calm him, the latter to make him euphoric. Thankfully, it worked.

He was still feeling good when he got to his hotel and started making phone calls. Pretty soon he didn't feel so good anymore. Most of his so-called "friends" wouldn't even talk to him. He could understand paranoia and caution—wanting to make sure it was really him they were talking to, and whether there was any word on him turning since they'd last spoken, but it wasn't that way at all. It was more the reaction just the mention of his name produced—instant freeze-out. It was *him* they didn't want to hear from, not some unremembered clown who could be a cop.

Cowboy couldn't figure it. He was sure he'd left all business here in the plus column, and except for a long-time-no-see wife or two, he couldn't think of anyone in Colombia who'd be unhappy to see him. What was going on?

The thought of those left-behind wives (were there two or three of them in Colombia—he couldn't remember) gave him an idea. Screw these *hijos de putas* who wouldn't give him the time of day, he'd just look up . . . what was her name again? Maria? No, that wasn't it. Marguerite! Right! Where did she live? He surveyed his mental map. Southwest corner of Colombia, Caqueta province, sitting on the southwestern shoulder of the Andes Cordillera Occidental—or Western Ridge to gringos. He pictured in his mind the air approach into the airfield first, and then the town's name came to him—Florencia! Marguerite from Florencia! How could he forget her? Puma-black hair and a temper to match, big brown eyes, and a great set of . . . but had he married her? Or had he just *promised* to marry her? Shit, his memory was a goddamned sieve when it came to women and his marital relationships with them. Oh, well, didn't matter much—either way he'd have some explaining to do. That was okay, because if he remembered correctly, Marguerite's brother was a hot-shot gangster—or at least fancied himself one. Always flashing a fat wad of bills, always trying to prove to Cowboy how important and powerful in the underworld he was. Full of stories about the tonnage of *cocaína* he moved every month and the hundreds of girls he bought and sold. Well, Cowboy thought as he headed back to the airport, it was time for old Jorge to show just how hot-shit he really was.

Damned if his memory wasn't so bad after all. He couldn't come up with the exact house number to tell the taxi driver, but he was able to direct the guy right to her door with a minimum of sidetracks. It was just after five in the afternoon when he pounded on the old wooden door, which meant Marguerite would be just waking up. Saloon singers aren't known to keep bankers' hours. The door was opened by a skinny, surly teenager. Cowboy's mind scrambled.

"Magdalena!" He cried out warmly, remembering the maid's name in the nick of time. He flashed her Cowboy Charming Smile #1—guaranteed irresistible to all females aged seven months to ninety-six years. Magdalena was unimpressed.

"Señor Cowboy," she said, sneering. "So, you have come back, like a dog who cannot find food anywhere else."

"I'm deliriously happy to see you, too, Magdalena. Still as friendly as ever, I see. Is *la bella señorita* awake yet? Why don't you rush off and tell her I'm here." Cowboy pushed past the recalcitrant maid and made his way to the living room. Magdalena eyed him sourly for a few seconds, then turned and shuffled off. He poured himself two fingers of Greek brandy and dropped into an overstuffed white chair. He only had time for a sip and a half before he had to take cover. Diving behind a couch to save the top of his head from a whizzing ashtray, Cowboy suddenly remembered why he'd last left this house. Marguerite had a better throwing arm than Reggie Jackson. And a voice louder than Howard Cosell's.

"*Maricón! Puerco!*" she shouted at the top of her lungs. "How dare you show your ugly face here, you goat-fucking whore-licker. I'll kill you with my own hands— I'll rip off your little raisin balls and stuff them in your ears!" She didn't seem happy to see him. Maybe she needed a bit of sweet talking.

"But precious . . . honey . . . you know I can't stay away from you for long. I'll *always* come back to you," he called from his fetal position under the couch. Small household items continued to catapult over his head, some of them crashing against the wall behind him, showering the floor with pieces of glass and clay. He could picture Magdalena standing by with a basket of ammunition, handing her a new projectile every time she threw one.

"Ha! You think I ever want to see your little worm-dick in my house again? You are dreaming! Go find a cat to lick your *cojones*—it's the only kind of pussy you know what to do with."

Cowboy tried another approach. "That little roll with Magdalena meant *nothing* to me, I swear. It was all her idea, anyway—before I knew what was happening she had her head in my pants. I couldn't stop her."

At that she screamed wordlessly, like Janet Leigh in the shower, and launched herself over the couch, like an ARVN leaping from a burning Huey. Ready for her kamikaze dive, Cowboy grabbed her wrists before her nails could rake the skin from his face, and rolled over on top of her. Her face was a vivid red, her mouth a full-auto spitting machine, and her legs kicked harder than a cornered Korean boxer. Cowboy was enjoying himself immensely. He got his lower torso between her knees after some concerted wriggling and deftly pulled the collar of her robe off her left shoulder with his mouth.

She bucked harder and tried to rip off his ears with her teeth. He pulled back out of her reach and nosed open the robe down to her navel. She screamed louder, but Cowboy noticed a distinct change in the character of her struggling; the focus of activity had changed from her legs to her pelvis. He now had her crotch pinned, along with her arms, and the fiercely convulsive arching of her back had knocked her breasts loose from the silken robe. They shook like coffee-colored Jell-O mounds as she fought him. He was on a roll now, he thought.

He knew just what to do, thanks to his newly reconfident memory. He circled her left nipple with his tongue and proceeded to bite his way eastward toward the other one. He tickled that one with his tastebuds for a few seconds, feeling it swell up and harden, and then nibbled at it gently with his front teeth. Her screams increased a few megahertz in frequency, pumped by her increasingly ragged breathing, and her pelvis seesawed wildly. She sure was a sucker for nipple-biting, Cowboy thought with smug pride.

Next he traced a saliva line up to her collarbone. He sank his teeth into the soft flesh of her neck, grinding with his lips and tongue, sucking in great mouthfuls of skin. A guttural moaning had risen up from Marguerite's throat, alternating one-on-one with her high-pitched shrieking. It was a sound Cowboy knew and loved. He was in like Flynn.

He lowered himself onto her until their heaving chests pressed against each other like airbags in an accordioned Mercedes. He covered her mouth with his and commenced cleaning her gums with his tongue. She sucked at him like she was a drowning woman and his throat was her lifeline, practically uprooting his tonsils. He released her arms, and she immediately went to work tearing his clothes off while his hands tossed aside the last folds of her robe. After her grindstone-sharpened nails had ripped his jockey shorts to threads, he reached behind her and palmed both her buttocks, guiding her up and over his twitching erection. It slid in easily, and she greeted its entry with renewed enthusiasm.

After fifty-seven minutes of furious grunting and thrusting, Cowboy's stamina gave out. He dropped in a jellied heap on top of Marguerite and exhaled so deeply he thought his lungs would implode from the vacuum.

"What, you are finished so soon?" she said with real disappointment. "But I was only just now getting warmed

80

up! I must go out and call in some boys from the street to finish the job."

Such a sweet girl, Cowboy thought; always knew when to say the right things. She's probably a scream at funerals. He had to expect as much from her, though—his misdeeds certainly weren't going to go unpunished. Steel yourself, Cowboy, old fella.

Sure enough, he felt a previously unaccounted-for hand tighten an unpromising grip around his balls. She squeezed them a bit, like priming lemons for the juicer, making sure Cowboy got the point. He did.

"So, Cowboy, *novio mio*, where have you been for so many months, eh? I was beginning to get worried."

"Oh, you know how it is." Cowboy chuckled uncomfortably. "Busy, busy, busy. You know what it's like when your services are in demand all over the place. People just keep offering you more money to do things, and I just couldn't turn them down. One job led to another, and before I knew it, *months* had gone by. I couldn't believe it! I said to myself, I'll bet sweet little Marguerite is just *beside* herself with worry, sitting tearfully by the window waiting for her man's plane to come in. So I just dropped everything I was doing, and hurried my ass back here. I knew you'd just be *ecstatic* to see me again, unhurt and ready to take up where we left off."

She sighed lightly in reply and gave his *pelotas* a few more playful squeezes.

"You tell such beautiful lies, Cowboy," she said to him. "Beautiful, but so lousy that not even Magdalena would believe them." She laughed heartily. He joined her in what he hoped was a reasonable facsimile of mirth. He didn't laugh well with his goodies in a vise.

"I guess that's true, sweetheart. I'm just too good a man to be a good liar."

"And that's the *worst* one you've ever told!"

He laughed for real at that.

"So, how long are you staying this time?" she asked.

He looked away. "I've got one more job to do. After that . . ." He couldn't finish the sentence. He'd suddenly lost his stomach for lying.

"Yes, I thought so. One more job." Her voice sounded sad but resigned. There was silence for a while. "Why did you come back at all, Cowboy? Right now I wish you'd stayed away. I liked it better when you were gone and I hated you. It is much simpler that way."

"I need to talk to Jorge," he said, still not looking at her. "I have some business for him if he wants it. Could mean lots of money if he can handle it."

"I guess I should go call him for you. Jorge likes business where he can make himself lots of money." She got up off the floor and pulled her robe tightly around herself. Without another word she walked out of the room.

Twenty minutes later, Jorge bounced through the front door. He was all smiles. Obviously Marguerite had told him what was up.

"Cowboy," he shouted, his arms wide. *"Mi amigo viejo! Como está?"* Anyone who could make him money was instantly his old friend.

"Cut the family reunion bullshit, Jorge—we both know you'd rather kill me than hug me. Let's just sit down and talk business."

The bearded Colombian laughed and took a seat opposite Cowboy. "True enough, my friend. My sister, she become *inconsolable* when you left. She didn't leave me alone. I almost came after you just to get away from her." He shook his head. "I tell you, don't do that again, *mi amigo*; I kill you for sure if you do that again." He gave his eyes a fiercely psychotic look—as pathetically fake as Cowboy's lies to Marguerite—to let Cowboy know he meant business.

"We can settle that score later, *maleante*—but first I need guns, ammunition, survival gear, and supplies for four in the jungle, and a plane with a two-thousand-kilometer range to drop it to them. Can you deliver?"

He shrugged confidently. "Of course. Side arms or assault weapons?"

"Both," Cowboy answered him. "I need four pistols—.45 caliber or 9mm self-loaders would be best; either Colts, Brownings, or Berettas. Figure a dozen clips per piece. Three assault rifles or submachine guns—Uzis, Sterling Mk IVs, MAC-10s, HK-91s, or at the very least M-16s, are preferred. Absolutely no AKs. Three hundred rounds per piece. All must be in factory-packed condition. And two special requests: one M-14 sniper rifle and one M-60 squad action weapon. Two or three twenty-round magazines for the M-14, and a couple of ammo belts for the '60. Also required are four fighting knives, a few dozen grenades, some C-4, a handful of Claymores, and maybe some gas cans for fun. I'll also need a videotape portapack, and a field radio. Think you can handle it?"

Jorge gave him the easy shrug again. "If the money's there, no problem."

"The money's here," Cowboy said, and pulled two rubber-banded wads of greenbacks from an inside pocket. "There's five thousand in each of those packages. That's a half payment. You'll get the other ten thousand before I step into the plane. Any problems?"

Jorge grinned widely and shook his head. "No problems at all, *amigo*, and it is truly a pleasure doing business with a man who knows just what he wants. No bullshitting around. I like that." He grinned again, and stuffed the money in his pockets. "I go make a phone call now, then we go for a ride." He left Cowboy alone.

He was back in less than a minute, and his grin was gone.

"Something doesn't smell right, *chico*. My man doesn't want to sell you *shit*. *Carajo*—he says the word has come down on your name, and four other names with yours. *Qué pasó, eh?*"

"Word has come down from *where*, Jorge?" What the fuck was going on here, Cowboy wondered.

"Word from above, Cowboy. From the big-ass gringos that run things in this part of the world. These are heavy people, who are used to having their words obeyed. If they say no guns for Cowboy and his friends, then *mi jefe* thinks he shouldn't sell you any guns. He thinks it's better for his health and future business prospects if he stays at home for this one."

Cowboy cursed. He had to figure something out; there was no way in hell he would leave Beeker, Rosie, Marty, and Harry stranded in Peru without weapons. He had been overconfident, and now he had to scramble to make good.

"What about you, Jorge? Do you jump when big-ass gringos snap their fingers?" It was button-pushing time, and Cowboy had a pretty good idea which of Jorge's buttons he had to push.

The Colombian laughed and reached into an inside jacket pocket. Pulling out a vial of cocaine the size of a roll of quarters, he said, "What do *you* think, Cowboy? What kind of man do you think Jorge Farina is, eh?"

Cowboy didn't answer him immediately, letting the man laugh some more in that deep, ho-ho-ho way some men use to show other men how bad-ass they are. He then spilled a healthy measure of white powder into the webbing of skin between the thumb and forefinger to his left hand and inhaled it cleanly with his nose. He passed the vial to Cowboy and then sat back on the couch to enjoy the drug's invigorating rush. Cowboy snorted an equal amount and handed back Jorge the vial.

84

"I think a man like you and a man like me can do some business, *hermano*," Cowboy said after a moment.

"Sure thing, I think we can, too. But tell me first," he asked, assuming a tone of confidentiality, "what sort of business are you in these days, eh? I'd like to know why these *mal hombres grandes* don't want anyone to sell you guns."

Cowboy leaned back, his body language broadcasting absolute confidence and relaxed trust in the man sitting across from him.

"I'm not really sure why the big heat's on me," he began casually. "But I think I have an idea. You see, *hermanito*, I've joined a security firm back in the States, and we've been hired to look after some people in Peru. Obviously, someone doesn't want us in the game and has put out the word to keep us weaponless."

"I would say, Cowboy, that you've chosen the wrong side to work for." He laughed again, and followed it with another noseful of coke.

The Texan grinned at him. "Yeah, well sometimes in this business, you don't get to choose who you work for—you kind of get drafted, if you know what I mean." Cowboy hoped that *almost* dropping the Agency's name would ease any of Jorge's fears about getting himself into trouble. It seemed to work.

"I understand. I think I can have what you need by tomorrow night. I know a man in the south who will lend us his plane for a small fee—it's an old one, a veteran of a few of your country's 'imperialistic wars,' but it can do the job. The equipment can be loaded and waiting for us by tomorrow. Is that all satisfactory?"

Cowboy nodded his head, feeding Jorge's ego with a mask of obvious respect and awe on his face. "Couldn't ask for a better arrangement, *compañero*." He hoped the unsubtle progression from friend to brother to partner wasn't

85

too clumsy for the ambitious Colombian. Cowboy thought he knew the guy pretty well, but it would be too easy to underestimate him.

"Then you won't take it wrong when I ask for an additional five thousand dollars for the tremendous risk I am undertaking." The man smiled wolfishly. Cowboy *had* underestimated him—but only in price.

"You are too good a businessman, my friend." Back to friend status. That was to let the bastard know he shouldn't push it too far.

Jorge laughed, proud of his skills. "So we have a deal, then. One more snort between friends and then we go celebrate our new partnership!"

And celebrate they did. Neither of them slept that night, going from restaurant to restaurant, nightclub to party to late-night club; filling their noses with stimulants and their stomachs with intoxicants. Cowboy didn't see Marguerite again that night, which saddened him a bit, but it was understandable. Jorge carefully steered all conversation away from that subject and smoothly kept the two of them from the club she worked at. Cowboy let him get away with it—he wasn't very good at dealing with emotional issues to begin with, and when he had other important business on his mind, he didn't want to deal with them at *all*. Foremost on his mind was the worry of who had put the blacklist out on the Black Berets. Whoever it was seemed to know their names and their plans, and the effectiveness of these shadow-men's influence over the local cocaine cowboys indicated they were indeed heavyweights. Well, if the story Jackie Simmons had told was true, then the people they would be hurting by helping this man Guiterrez were certainly heavyweights—the national government of Peru, most of the country's big shots, CIA renegades, and the local drug mafia. Big stuff, all right.

He hoped that didn't mean big ugliness for the Black Berets, but with the way things had been going, he was afraid it would.

Just before noon, Jorge drove Cowboy to a small airfield a few miles south of Florencia. Waiting for them there was a friend of the Colombian's, already revving up a single-engine Cessna that would take them the three hundred miles south into the Amazonian jungle where the Peru-bound plane awaited them. Cowboy was barely conscious by then and managed to get a bit of sleep on the flight down. He poked his head up groggily when the small craft landed roughly on an asphalt strip carved out of the dense, rain-forest foliage.

They were greeted by an old guy with dry, sun-tanned skin, a big bushy mustache, and rotten teeth. Cowboy was introduced and, since he was still half-asleep, promptly forgot the character's name. While Jorge and the old guy gibbered away in Indy 500-speed Spanish, Cowboy tried to jolt himself awake, first with a dose from Jorge's vial, then with some jumping-in-place calisthenics. Nothing worked until he saw the plane he'd be flying.

To put it mildly, the thing was a wreck. It was an old C-47, camo-painted and dusty, sitting under a ragged canopy off the end of the runway. The old guy, still yammering nonstop, ran up to the thing, kicking the tires and dusting off selected spots on the fuselage. He seemed proud of the old crate.

"Does the fucking thing still *fly*?" Cowboy asked Jorge.

Jorge looked hurt. "But of course, *amigo*. Jaime wouldn't lend it to us if it didn't. He is my old, old friend." He put his arm around the old guy's shoulders, and the two of them grinned like mongoloids.

"Right," Cowboy said under his breath. Louder, he asked, "When was the last time it was in the air?"

87

Jorge translated for the old guy, who answered with an unconvincingly sincere burst of *español*.

"Jaime says not more than a few years. It used to make regular runs from here across the Gulf to Texas and Oklahoma, loaded with marijuana. But then they got smaller and faster ones to do the job—so *El Bandito* was retired."

"*El Bandito*, eh?" Cowboy did a pilot's walk around the C-47's undercarriage. It looked like Korean War vintage and probably had seen some Vietnam action as well—more than likely in the Laotian or South Vietnamese air forces, who were gifted with a bunch of C-47s by the U.S. Government in the early sixties. The twin 1200-horsepower engines looked tired but workable, newly applied lubrication dripping profusely from their dented prop collars.

"Any armament on this thing?" Cowboy called to the two Colombians, who were now snorting chumily from Jorge's bottomless canister.

"Jaime says, regretfully no. It was all removed before he bought *El Bandito* at a CIA rummage sale."

Great, Cowboy thought to himself, looking sourly at the patched-up tail section. The skin looked like painted-over Swiss cheese. He hoped his trip wouldn't produce more holes; it didn't look like it could take any more. He walked away from the thing shaking his head.

"Come, Cowboy," Jorge said with brotherly affection. "Let's go up to the *hacienda* where you can check the cargo and we can all have some dinner. Then, after they've fueled the plane up, we can take off for the sky." He made a plane noise and buzzed his hand past Cowboy's face.

"You're coming *with* me?" Cowboy was surprised. He didn't think Jorge would want anything to do with this once the heat went on.

"But of course! Do you think I would miss any of this action? It promises to be great fun!" He seemed incredulous at Cowboy's assumption that he would stay behind. Did Jorge think he had to show Cowboy how macho he was, or had Cowboy underestimated him *again*?

The guns up in the house also looked tired but usable. They were M-16s wrapped in a native blanket, probably pinched from a National Guard armory. There was even an M-60 for Applebaum, and it needed a cleaning, which would keep Marty happily busy for hours. The pistols were Browning Hi-Powers with an Argentinian manufacturer's stamp. The finish didn't gleam like the Belgian or U.S.-licensed models, but they functioned up to snuff. He test fired the lot off the back porch, and beyond the obvious problems of misaligned sights, they seemed fine—no pitting in the barrels, no corrosion. He nodded his approval to Jorge, who clapped him happily on the back.

Dinner was a freshly caught, catfishlike thing from a nearby river, washed down with too many bottles of white wine. Coffee, strong and sweet, followed, sipped slowly between much full-auto conversation between Jaime and Jorge. Cowboy writhed itchily in his seat. It was almost eight before he finally was able to drag Jorge to the waiting *El Bandito*.

The ignition coughed several times and needed the encouragement of Jaime's men yanking on the propeller blades before it caught. Only after things started spinning smoothly and the wrenching jolts of the balky Pratt and Whitneys settled into a rhythmic lurch did Cowboy loose the breath he'd been holding in his lungs. Maybe this old thing *will* get off the ground after all, he thought with a laugh. Jorge certainly was into it—he was hanging his head out the co-pilot's window, hooting like a wild man at the ground crew pulling the blocks away from *El Bandito*'s wheels.

Cowboy increased the fuel feed and felt the rear landing gear jump in anticipation. *El Bandito* was hot to trot.

Cowboy patted the hood of the flight console like a jockey encouraging his mount.

"Nothing like being back in the saddle again, eh, old boy? Wait'll we get up there—it'll be even *better*."

Cowboy eased off the fuel feed and released the wheel brakes. The plane rolled forward slowly, as though it were pulling at the leash like a dog anxious as hell to get out the front door. He put *El Bandito* into a tight right turn onto the runway and waved at the prop-blasted figure of Jaime holding his hat with one hand and waving with the other. His grin was miles wide. Jorge was still hanging out of his window, bellowing his guts out.

"I'm glad *you* two guys are enjoying yourselves."

After a moment's pause at the starting line, Cowboy opened up the throttle and started the charge down the runway. *El Bandito* growled happily and did as he was told. They roared down the asphalt between the burning barrels of fuel-soaked rags marking the edges of safety. The darkening jungle whipped past and grew up at the end of the runway in front of them. Cowboy had the throttle at full feed, the stick pulled practically into his lap—it was all up to *El Bandito* now. The old crate hesitated for a moment, suddenly uncertain of his *real* desire to get off the safe ground again, and then, just before it looked like they were into the wall of jungle, he did it. It was like he'd said to himself, "Aw, what the fuck," and reached for the sky. They were airborne.

"All right, my man!" Cowboy shouted. Jorge whooped a few in agreement. It was truly a miracle.

Cowboy pulled up on the C-47's nose until they reached three thousand feet and leveled off. He pointed the craft in an almost due south direction and locked the wheel in place. The easy part was over. Now it was time to think about what might be waiting for them in Peru and what

90

they'd be able to do about it. Not a damn lot. He turned to his co-pilot.

"Hey, *caballero*! Let's see that little bottle of yours one more time."

It was going to be a long night. He'd better make the best of it.

# 7

Beeker, Applebaum, Harry, and Rosie huddled in the bushes at the edge of the Peruvian altiplano. Jackie sat nearby, her body totally enveloped in a brightly colored, handwoven blanket. She was shivering but silent. She had tried complaining for a while, but when all she got were offers of shared body heat, she gave up. It had gotten cold after sunset, as it does all year round at altitudes in the three-thousand-kilometer range. Cowboy wasn't due for another hour at least, and they all were already growing impatient. Except Beeker, who had curled up and gone to sleep. That had always driven Rosie nuts. Damn Indian could fall asleep in the middle of a firefight—and had, many times, in Nam—without a struggle.

It had taken a while for the brooding black man to cool down. The humiliating scuffle earlier with Applebaum still burned in his craw, but he had set it aside for redressing later. He didn't like the way the squirrelly cat was trying to make time at his expense with the lady—who he was still pretty sure was hot for him. There was no mistaking the looks she gave him, the smiles, the touches. He'd get his shot at her later. He wasn't worried.

What did worry him was the sudden appearance on the scene, two hours before sunset, of local military personnel. They'd heard them before they saw them—multiple chopper blades coming in from the distance. They'd all looked at each other and formed the same word simultaneously in their heads: *Hueys!* No one had to say a thing. It was a sound they all knew too well.

A formation of three Peruvian Army UH-1Hs passed overhead. They were flying slowly but purposefully in a northeasterly direction. They appeared fully weighted, probably airlifting nine or ten troopers each, and from the way their door gunners lounged over their starboard-mounted M-60s, they appeared not to be looking for anything. Not yet.

It worried Boone just the same. Was this a routine patrol, or were the locals alerted to the Black Beret's presence? He supposed—given the country's political climate—a military presence in a region suspected of being an anti-government hotbed should be expected. Just the same, they all instantly proceeded with the utmost care; if the *guardia* weren't looking already, they didn't want to give them a reason to start. They felt helpless out there— four men and a woman without a weapon between them. Boone knew he'd feel much better after Cowboy's drop.

An hour before sunset, Beeker ordered them to break camp. They packed up what they would need for the drop and stowed the rest. Beeker led the way through a path he'd cut earlier in the underbrush, winding downward to the ancient Inca footpath that would take them to the DZ. Jackie followed immediately behind him, then Harry, Applebaum, and Rosie, all in a single column.

It wasn't easy going. The path was narrow, sometimes less than a foot in width, and rocky. That afternoon's rain shower had left the surface slick and treacherous, particularly bothersome when the path clung to a cliffside overlooking a drop of hundreds of feet. Add to that the constant sky-watch needed to warn of approaching helicopters, and you had one hour of exhausting work. Jackie whined the entire time and fell into an immobile heap when they reached their destination. Then they waited, as the darkness closed in. They heard the *whap-whap-whap* of distant choppers a few more times as night fell, but they never came close enough for visual contact. Beeker assigned Rosie to stand watch for the next hour and told Applebaum and Pappathanassiou to get some rest. He drifted off into a shallow sleep, jerking out periodically at the sound of chopper blades and Marty's annoying cackle. He and Harry were too keyed up to sleep and were spending their time gabbing—or at least Applebaum was—about improbable recent adventures involving a platoon of New Orleans whores and enough liquor to irrigate Death Valley. Beeker tried not to listen.

The Peruvian Air Force HueyCobra gunships jumped on Cowboy's tail about one hundred and fifty klicks north of the DZ. There were two of them. They came out of nowhere and settled in like patient wasps, about two hundred feet to his rear, one at three o'clock, one at nine o'clock. They seemed in no hurry at all, secure in the superiority of their maneuverability and firepower. They were waiting for the word to swoop in for the kill, and perhaps an opportunity to mix some pleasure with their business. Cowboy felt like an elephant rider at the Kentucky Derby. His stomach twisted painfully.

"Give *El Bandito* some juice, *amigo*! Let's give these *maricones* something to chase after." Jorge was cranked for a good fight. He was hopping up and down in his seat like an impatient child, checking their pursuers out the side window. He produced an Ingram MAC-10 from a flight bag under his seat and readied it for action by fixing the folding stock in place.

"First of all, Jorge, if I give this old guy any more juice, he'll drown. And second of all, that garden hose you got there ain't gonna do you much good. It don't have the range or the stopping power. You may's well be spitting at 'em.''

It was the truth, but Jorge didn't give a shit. He grinned, kissed the bolt on the submachine gun's top, and drove a ten-inch clip into the handgrip. Cowboy had never cared much for the Big MAC; it was square, stubby, and ugly—like a cookie box with a nozzle—and was only good for uncontrolled short-range room spraying. He especially hated the twenty pounds of trigger pressure needed to get it going; what kind of control could you have with that? Hotshots like Jorge, though, loved the weapon because it packed small and produced an impressive pyrotechnic display. Nothing like emptying a forty-round magazine in about the time it takes you to sneeze. A man's got to have his fun, Cowboy supposed—but if a man wants to take care of business there are plenty of better weapons to choose from.

Jorge wasn't about to be convinced, though. He was war-whooping like a hyperactive twelve-year-old and waving the MAC around with his right hand like a toy pistol. He was having some serious fun.

Cowboy, on the other hand, wasn't having any fun at all. He pushed forward on the stick to tuck the plane closer in to the river he was following—the Urubamba—but he knew that it wouldn't really make much of a difference. *El Bandito* was a sitting duck for the two HueyCobras on his tail. It was only a matter of time before they'd poke him out of the sky—and the time was all *theirs*.

Cowboy was all too familiar with the capabilities of the AH-1S, having flown the chopper dozens of times in Nam. It was a funny little ship, only thirty-six inches wide at the cockpit, with the pilot sitting above and behind the navigation/gunnery officer. Its impressive array of armaments—including a multi-barrel 7.62mm Minigun and a 40mm grenade launcher in remote-control turrets, and side-mounted pods carrying seventy-six 2.75-inch rockets— qualified the HueyCobra as airborne anti-tank artillery, but that didn't mean it couldn't bring down a lumbering old C-47. For a moment, Cowboy let himself dream that he was sitting in the cockpit of a Hughes AH-64, the Army's vicious new attack helicopter half again faster than the HueyCobra and armed with the deadly new laser-guided Hellfire Missile System. He could almost see the target gunships in the sight that ship could project onto his eye, ready to fix them with his laser designator. . . .

But the truth was, he was flying an unarmed antique whose nine-lives account was already pathetically overdrawn. No, reality wasn't looking good at all.

Beeker was the first to hear Cowboy's noisy approach. He had been at his forward DZ position for more than three hours—cold, cramped, impatient, and worried. But he felt only relief when the distant sounds of a rickety old Gooney Bird reached his ears. Beeker smiled. Where the *hell* had Cowboy scraped up an old '47 for himself? But the smile quickly froze on his face—something was wrong.

He could see the plane now, coming in over the Vilcanota River valley—coming in too low and too fast. He'd *never* make the drop that way. Then Beeker saw the two insectlike gunships on the transport's tail, running lights flashing angrily, their pug noses pointed belligerently downward. Those HueyCobras weren't up there playing tag. They meant business.

Cowboy caught the frantic flashes of Beeker's infrared signal in his binocular viewer as he zoomed over the DZ.

"Well," he said to himself, "looks like this one's gonna be a two-pass drop—let's just hope it's the cargo that gets dropped and not the plane."

He knew getting out of this one would take some fancy-shit flying, possibly the fanciest he'd ever attempted. Simply, he had to shake these two bastards off his ass if he wanted to complete the drop and get his butt out of there. It really wasn't as impossible as it sounded; he had an idea that might work. It was a maneuver he'd learned from the pilot of a three-minigun-equipped C-47 he'd known in Nam (the Gooney Bird gunships were called Puff the Magic Dragons back there), involving tipping the ship over on its side and circling the ground target. He was hoping it would be enough to confuse the insects on his tail. But just as he was trying to hook a left-hand turn around a four-thousand-plus kilometer mountain peak, to take a second pass over the DZ, they started shooting at him.

They'd either gotten an order from somewhere or else they'd just both decided it was high time to down him. They both opened up with their 7.62s at the same time. Their aim wasn't too good, but when the target was that big and that close, how could you miss? They didn't. Cowboy could feel the plane shudder slightly as it took some rounds. The old boat hesitated a bit but made the turn okay and roared back toward the DZ. The Cobras kept peppering him with their miniguns, whizzing their every-third-round green tracers past *El Bandito*'s wings. Then a white streak caught the left corner of Cowboy's vision—one of the Cobras had loosed a 2.75-inch rocket at them.

"Hang on, Jorge," Cowboy shouted to his companion. "I'm gonna put *El Bandito* through the wringer!"

But the Colombian wasn't listening. He had leaped out of the co-pilot's seat and was scrambling back into the cargo bay. Clutching the MAC in his right hand, he used his left to spin the release on the portside air-drop hatch. Yanking it free, he leaned out the opening with a yelp, and sprayed one of the Cobras with staccato bursts of 9mm

97

parabellum fire. He was wide by a few dozen yards—one-handed full-auto Ingram fire is less accurate than a blind man trying to piss into a keyhole—but it encouraged the other pilots to give them more room. Jorge shouted insanely and waved his weapon. Next the guy would beat his chest and yodel like Tarzan, Cowboy thought.

It was the second 2.75 whooshing past his window—close enough for him to see the blue stripes at the two ends of the seventeen-inch cylinder—that convinced him it was time to rattle these Peruvian pussies. He shouted a warning to Jorge and wrenched the flap controller to his left. *El Bandito* spun into a wild roll. Jorge howled his approval.

Beeker watched with controlled horror as the old C-47 headed back toward the DZ for another pass. He could see the gunship's green tracer threads piercing the Gooney Bird's wings. He knew that the old crate couldn't take too many rounds and stay in the air. There was no way that Cowboy was gonna pull this one out. . . .

Then something happened that brought a smile to his lips. Maybe there *was* some hope after all—he should know better than to write Cowboy off before he was dead and buried.

The C-47's wings spun wickedly in a clockwise direction, and its nose jumped to the right. Like a wire-directed model plane, the ship jerked into a 180-degree turn that caught the Cobras completely by surprise. The chopper pilots panicked, thinking the *loco* in the Gooney Bird had decided to ram them. They scattered like hounds from an angry boar and circled back warily from opposite ends of *El Bandito*'s seesawing wingtips. Their minigun bursts became more erratic and halfhearted—they were obviously scared and confused by the insanely unpredictable pilot of the C-47. For all they knew, he would throw himself into their rotor blades just for the hell of it.

Cowboy pressed his advantage. He obviously had them on the defensive, so he did what any hopelessly outgunned, outnumbered soldier should do. He acted even more outrageously insane. Beeker watched with awe. It was a ridiculous sight: two heavily armed gunships running chicken from an unarmed old cargo boat. He wished the video camera was down here instead of up there.

The C-47 dropped suddenly, nose to the ground, spiraled out to the left, then waggled its wings and jacked itself straight up into what looked like a certain stall. The HueyCobras moved in cautiously from above when the '47 dipped down, and jumped off when the plane reared up at them. One of the choppers dropped back and below while the other pulled up and creeped along Cowboy's spine. The one above maneuvered itself to the left, so it could look down and into the C-47's cockpit and lead the plane with the leash made by its minigun tracers. The one behind dropped off to the right and lowered its tail like an angry bumblebee poised to sting.

And then something amazing happened.

The tip of Cowboy's right wing peeled off, chopped free by a wild sweep from the leading gunship's turret-mounted miniguns. Seconds later, the rear-tailing Cobra loosed a 2.75 in a spray of smoke and flames. The C-47 shuddered painfully, and fell into a sweeping left-hand turn. The missile—lucky for Cowboy, the dumb, point-it-and-shoot variety—zoomed harmlessly past the Gooney Bird's belly and impacted violently with the tail section of the forward chopper. At almost the same instant, the debris shot off Cowboy's wing dropped into the lower gunship's spinning rotor. The upper one exploded in a blinding flash of flame and black smoke. The lower one flipped end-over-end three times and then dropped like a lead-filled bird to the ground. Beeker felt the vibrations of the crash before he saw the flash-lit column of smoke billow up from behind a nearby hill.

It would've been perfect if Cowboy had waltzed away from the dogfight and been able to make the drop. Miraculous. But he didn't. Beeker could tell the plane was in serious trouble, dropping fast and desperately searching for a place to put down. But this wasn't the best neighborhood for forced landings. It was obvious Cowboy was having difficulty keeping the plane in the air. Beeker could see the struggle going on, and he could also see that Cowboy was losing. It would only be a matter of seconds.

The plane was dropping like an overloaded express elevator. There was no way Cowboy was going to keep the thing airborne for much longer. Clearing the altiplano's eastern edge, where the ground dropped quickly toward the river valley, gave him some breathing room, but it was only postponing the inevitable. Beeker ran to the terraced cliffside for a visual fix on where the C-47 would go down.

Standing behind a crumbling, Inca-era stone wall, Beeker watched the plane tumbling toward the earth. Obviously, Cowboy had realized that the only hope for a survivable landing lay in the water cushion of the Vilcanota River. That was where the crippled Gooney Bird was headed, and with a little luck, it would make it. And if Cowboy still had enough control over the plane's angle of descent, maybe the plane would skim to a landing instead of nose-diving into the riverbed.

The plane's belly hit the surface of the water a few klicks northeast of Beeker's position. It shook and bounced up like a side-armed rock skating across a swimming hole. It came down again a couple of short seconds later, slower and easier, raising a trail of spray only half as high as the one from the initial contact. Then it bounced up again, not high at all, and touched the water again. The plane's air

100

speed had dropped perceptibly. Cowboy cut the engines and leveled his flaps. He was down.

Beeker couldn't believe his eyes. The C-47 was hydroplaning to a stop on the river, taking to the water like a flying boat. His astonished, dropped-jaw look transformed into a smile.

"Fucking-A Cowboy!" he muttered to himself, shaking his head with admiration. He turned around to look for his companions and saw the four of them running in a scattered line toward him. He waved at them to join him at the cliffside, motioning that everything was A-OK. When he turned back to the river, the situation had changed completely.

The C-47's wings were wobbling frantically. Cowboy was trying to keep them stable with his flaps, but the crippled old boat wasn't paying much attention. The tipless right wing was the first to hit the water, grazing the surface and lifting a trail of white spray. Then it came up, but the left one seesawed down and buried itself in the river. The fuselage reared up and twisted to its left, like it was riding the wing tip like a water ski. Had it been moving any faster the plane would've cartwheeled forward and smacked up for sure. But it was going slow enough so that its weight was overcoming its forward momentum. It was dropping back down on its belly, when the submerged wing tip hit a rock. Then it was all over.

The wing wanted to come to a full stop, but the fuselage wanted to keep going. The wing won. The plane pitched over forward and plunged its nose into the river. It stood like that for an eternal instant—head and shoulders under water, tail section reaching for the moon—and then flopped down hard on its bruised belly.

Rosie's voice came from behind Beeker. "Jesus damn *Christ!*" He said between panting breaths.

101

Beeker wasted no time. When Harry, Applebaum, and—lastly, complainingly—Jackie reached the cliff's edge, he spoke.

"We've got to get down there to see if Cowboy's okay, and to get the weapons away from here before the whole fucking Peruvian Army comes down on our asses. Harry, you take Runt and Jackie and head down that south trail there." He pointed to a spot a couple of hundred feet away where there was a break in the terrace walls. Harry nodded curtly. "Rosie and I will take this trail up here. We'll meet on the riverbank just where the Gooney Bird is sitting. Hurry, but be careful on the trail. I don't want any more casualties."

"Got it." Harry nodded again.

"Let's move." Beeker said, and turned toward the trail.

The way down was tough going. This trail was no better than the one they'd taken earlier, and the near-total darkness made it almost impossible to traverse safely. Beeker was pushing his speed to the limit, and at a couple of points—feet sliding, stumbling over rocks—he thought for sure he'd pushed it too far. He could tell from the scrambling and cursing behind him that Rosie wasn't doing any better. But since Boone wasn't tumbling over any cliffs, either, they were both ahead of the game. For now.

It was a good hour before they cleared the down-winding path and entered the dense vegetation that jacketed the river. Beeker and Rosie plunged into the triple-canopy darkness and stumbled to a halt. They couldn't see a thing.

"Shit, man," Rosie said, "we're back in fucking Nam." The jungle here was indistinguishable from any they had crawled through ten years earlier and thousands of miles away. A jungle is a jungle, no matter where the hell it is.

Beeker didn't waste time discussing the matter. He started reaching around blindly at the edges of the trail, groping for some recently cut bamboo stalks. He should be able to find some lying around dead enough to burn and light their way to the riverbank. He was right. He found one about two feet long, and wrapped an end with some dead leaves that he scooped from the ground. It took a couple of matches to get it going, but once it came alight, the trail opened up before them.

"Let's go!" he said to Rosie, and took off at a run into the jungle. The torch flickered uncertainly but threw enough light for the two of them to reach the silt-and-pebble bank within five minutes. A quick look downriver told them the C-47 was located a couple of hundred yards north of them, but a sound from above made them both freeze.

"Fucking Phantoms!" Rosie said, and dived back for the protection of the underbrush. Beeker dropped the torch into the river and followed him. Obviously, the gunships had called for help before they went down, and two tough-looking F-4E fighters had been sent in from a nearby airfield. They were circling overhead, fixed on the half-submerged Gooney Bird, swooping and soaring like a pair of bats.

"We've got to get down there and see if Cowboy's all right! If we keep close enough to the foliage, we should be able to get near the plane without those boys upstairs seeing us. They're probably too busy watching the plane to check the banks, anyway."

They were off, keeping as close to the protective foliage as they could, running in a half-crouch over the stones and grasslike brush that marked the division between jungle and riverbank. Between the exertion of the running and the fear that gripped his heart, Beeker was barely able to breathe. When he came up even with the downed Gooney Bird he stopped and inhaled desperately, like a marathoner just past the finish line. Rosie joined him. They both stood with their hands on their hips, mouths and nostrils sucking the thick tropical air, eyes searching the crash site for any kind of movement.

The C-47 sat silent and motionless in the water, the river's current lapping around the badly dented fuselage. Neither Beeker nor Rosie spoke a word—the only sounds were their tortured breathing, the jungle's night screams, and the roaring of the Phantom jets overhead. There was no sign of life. Beeker's stomach dropped into his crotch.

Nothing happened for an eternity of seconds.

Suddenly, there was a voice from the jungle behind them. A familiar voice.

"Well, now," the familiar voice said, "it shore is nice of you boys to come meet me. After a landing like that, a man likes to see some friendly faces."

Beeker whirled. It was too dark to make out much, but there was a white-clad figure sprawled on a rock about a hundred feet upriver.

"My god, Cowboy," Beeker said, "I thought for sure you'd hotdogged your last Gooney Bird."

"Yeah," Rosie joined in, "and we were just trying to figure out how many wives we'd have to call and break the bad news to. Looks like you saved us the trouble."

Cowboy laughed uncaringly. But when Beeker got close enough to see him he could tell the Texan hadn't gotten away completely unscathed. There was an ugly gash on his forehead, and blood was dripping from the end of it down his temple. It was colorful but probably not too serious.

"Are you okay?" Beeker asked, standing over him.

"Hell, yeah," Cowboy answered with a shrug. "That was only a little tumble I took—weren't no worse than falling in the shower. The swim across is what almost got me. Never did care much for water."

Cowboy sat on the rock, sprawled on his left side, patting something next to him with his hand. Beeker thought at first that he was laid out that way because of an injury he'd sustained in the crash. But now he could see that the pilot had something on the rock that he seemed very concerned about. Some of the weapons he was supposed to have dropped?

"What d'ya got there?" Beeker asked him.

"Oh, just a little something I salvaged from my co-pilot's luggage," he answered guiltily.

Beeker leaned over and looked. Spread out on the rock were three sandwich-sized plastic bags bulging with white paste. It probably had been white powder before the water had gotten to it. Cowboy was patting all three of them in sequence, trying to squeeze the milky water out of the open tops of the baggies without losing any of the paste.

"Fucking cocaine!" Beeker cried out. "Of all the things you could've pulled from that plane, you had to grab the fucking drugs first! Cowboy, I oughta punch your nose so damn hard you'll never be able to get anything up there again!"

Behind him Rosie started laughing hysterically.

"Aw, c'mon, Beek!" Cowboy was getting an alarmingly Applebaum-like tone in his voice. It didn't suit him. "We can go back and get the guns later, but this shit don't keep too well in the water. It was a logical choice—you woulda done the same thing!"

"Not a chance," Beeker said. Stepping over the protesting Texan, he scooped up all three bags of coke and threw them into the river.

"Aw, shit, Beeker," Cowboy said, practically crying. "Why'd you have to go and do that?"

Beeker leaned over the prone pilot until their faces were inches apart. "And I oughta throw *you* in after 'em!"

Cowboy shut his mouth and pouted. Rosie kept laughing. Beeker stalked off angrily toward the jungle.

They were in *deep* shit now.

# 8

The Peruvian Air Force Phantom jets continued to circle the C-47 like two vultures waiting for their prey to die. And if that wasn't bad enough, the F-4Es were soon joined by other, more worrisome carrion birds—troop-filled helicopters.

Three slow-moving Hueys led by two Cobra gunships arrived on the scene not five minutes after Harry, Marty, and Jackie did—and not thirty seconds after they'd all taken cover in the jungle.

Though his face remained impassive, Beeker burned furious inside. Any chance of them recovering the weapons from the downed C-47 had just been killed. Now, getting their asses clear of the area became their main objective. They had jungle-trained troops on their trail, and no weapons to defend themselves with. All they could do was run, and hope the Peruvians wouldn't catch them before they reached safety somewhere. Beeker didn't like that kind of setup at all. But it was all he had. He needed time to think, to plan; but right now he had to get more distance between his party and the platoon of camouflaged troopers jumping from their Hueys not two hundred yards from his position. With some distance, maybe he'd get time to think.

"Move out," he whispered to the rest.

"What?" Jackie demanded indignantly.

106

Beeker stopped in his tracks. "I said *move out*! We've got to clear this area before those guys figure out we're here." He couldn't believe he was explaining his orders to this woman. He did it without thinking.

"And what about the camera? The whole reason we're here is to tape this interview and we can't do that without the camera! You can't just *leave* it there. You've got to go out there and *get* it!"

That was it. Beeker had had too much. He lost his cool. Jackie Simmons was dead meat. He was going to rip her pretty face off her skull, right now. . . .

But Harry's bulk intervened. The Greek's massive back filled Beeker's vision and snapped the fixation his killer instinct had attached to Jackie's face. It was just in time.

"You heard the man's orders, Jackie." Harry's voice was calm and even. "He's the team leader, and he gives the orders. We listen. That commando platoon out there means that whatever's on that plane is lost to us. And if we stick around this area much longer, they're bound to find us, too. Our only chance is to get the hell out of here and make alternate arrangements when we're safely away."

Jackie didn't say anything, but Harry didn't wait for an answer. He moved off up the trail, with Applebaum and Rosie falling in behind him. Beeker stood stone-still, staring at her without saying a word. Making it clear that she wasn't happy with any of this, she finally relented and joined the trail. Beeker watched her go and took one last look at the river activity.

Two of the Hueys now sat on the riverbank, rotors slowing. The bulk of the commando platoon was sprawled lazily on the rocks. Obviously, they believed no one else was around for them to be on the lookout for. Over the river the two Cobras were training their high-candlepower spotlights on the C-47. The third Huey was moving in over the downed plane's cockpit, lowering a single trooper onto it by rope. Within minutes they would find the cargo and the single dead body of someone who obviously wasn't the pilot. Then they'd come looking for the pilot. Beeker turned away and headed up the trail.

He caught up with the rest of them where the jungle gave way to the rocky climb to the altiplano. Jackie was speaking to the group but stopped quickly when Beeker broke cover. The men looked tense and annoyed. Jackie looked affronted, like a servant had just given her some lip. Beeker could guess what had been going on; Jackie obviously presumed on her power over his men and figured she could get them to go back for her camera against Beeker's orders. They would do no such thing, of course. Beeker ignored the tension that was hanging in the air like a pungent fart cloud and started giving orders.

"Harry," he began, and was gratified to see instant recognition of his authority in the Greek's dark eyes, "take Jackie back up to the camp and prepare for a quick exit. Wait for us there. If we're not there by sunup, hit the road with the Land-Rover and don't look back until you make the rendezvous with Guiterrez's men."

Harry nodded and turned to go.

"Going back for the camera, are you?" Jackie said with a victorious smile.

"No," Beeker answered coldly. "We're going back to secure some weapons and maybe a platoon's worth of Peruvian scalps."

Applebaum giggled stupidly at Jackie's horrified reaction, while Rosie just grunted. Harry took the woman's arm and pulled her up the trail. When they were out of sight, Beeker turned to Applebaum, Cowboy, and Boone.

"Here's what's happening. Those Marines down there are going to be bloodhounding us soon, so it's up to us to launch the first strike, hitting them before they're expecting anything. We have to isolate a squad of them, take them out, retrieve their weapons, and retire quickly. I don't want to engage the entire platoon—that'll just bring more down on us. I want a quick, clean, noiseless bump-and-run. Now, let's get back to the riverbank and see what those clowns are up to."

Down by the drowned Gooney Bird everything had changed. The Peruvian commandos had obviously discovered the lack of a pilot in the plane, either dead or alive. They'd also discovered the cargo of weapons, which naturally meant a reception committee for the drop, which naturally meant a high probability of armed hostile forces in the area. The platoon captain had ordered a defensive perimeter set up, and the troopers who'd been lazing about when Beeker had last checked them were now alert and watchful.

Inside the perimeter, there was a talkative powwow in progress. The officer in charge—identifiable by his mirrored shades, starched cap, and precisely creased uniform—was animatedly briefing his three squad leaders and five chopper pilots. From his hand gestures Beeker could deduce that the officer was doing just what he hoped he would (and probably just what he would've done in the man's position). He was splitting the platoon into three squad-size parties and sending them up three different trails to look for the pilot and whoever else might be in the area. The choppers were to fan out overhead, providing illumination, observation, and firepower. Probably, Beeker figured, the platoon commander would put himself in one of the Hueys and maintain radio contact with his three squads, directing the operation from above. When the officer dismissed his men, Beeker knew he'd figured right.

He'd seen enough. They only had a couple of minutes to prepare the ambush. He hand-signaled "move out" to his men and ran light-footed up the trail. Rosie, Cowboy, and Applebaum fell in behind him at five-yard intervals, each in their turn checking the perimeter of Marines for any signs that their presence had been detected. So far, so good.

Beeker brought his men back to a spot on the trail he'd marked in his head earlier. It offered the best terrain for a quick, silent ambush by an outnumbered party of unarmed men. The trail dog-legged around a large rock and dipped into a depression just past the turn, effectively cutting off visual contact between the first and and last men in the column. The trail was narrow and offered heavy cover on both sides, so that a good ambusher would be close enough to spit-shine the ambushee's boots before the poor slob knew what was going on. Beeker counted on the fact that the patrol wouldn't be expecting an ambush executed by pros. With that maximum surprise, and the Black Berets' proven skill, there was a good chance they could pull it off. A good chance.

"This is the setup," Beeker began, crouched back Japanese-style, butt by his heels and knees up by his shoulders. "We're going to wait until the column is broken by that rock there, four on this side and three not yet around it. Marty, you take out the rear man first, then Rosie the man in front of him, and Cowboy the third guy just by the rock. I'm going to rig a bait line up the trail fifteen or so yards—right there—to keep the four forward men moving. I want a pit right here in the depression, some punji sticks rigged up in it, and a trip line right here to make sure they fall in. Cowboy and Rosie, start digging.

110

Marty, find me two vines; one about fifteen yards long, another about six. I'll find some bamboo sticks to sharpen. If you need my Sting for anything, just whistle. Any questions?"

Three silent shakes of the head.

"Good. Get to work."

They had just over fifteen minutes of setup time. They only needed twelve. Beeker heard Applebaum's whistle signaling the column's approach. Other than the churning hum of the choppers circling uselessly above the triple canopy, it was the only sound in the jungle. The jungle had a way of knowing when something was happening; it sensed it, the way a mother senses something's wrong with her children. And when it senses something wrong, the jungle covers itself with a blanket of silence and waits. Good jungle fighters learn to hear that silence and prepare themselves for an ambush. Beeker counted on the fact that these Peruvians weren't good jungle fighters. Was he underestimating them?

Beeker saw a sweeping shaft of light skim the trail before he saw the point man turn the corner. He lay there on his belly, motionless, his legs spread out behind him in the brush, his chin in the dirt, his eyes inches from the trail. Insects were crawling up his trouser legs, and a rock point was digging into his ribs, but he didn't notice. His mind told him he was back in Vietnam, and it told him he was dead jungle foliage. He was barely breathing, and his eyes were open just enough to see his approaching victim. He watched and waited. He thought of nothing.

The point man was wearing camo-fatigues and a dark-colored beret. His M-16 sling was over his right shoulder, and his right elbow clamped the weapon's plastic stock firmly to his waist. His right hand gripped the pistollike butt, and his index finger rested not on the trigger, but against the thin metal trigger guard beneath it. He was

111

holding a bulky flashlight in his left hand and was sweeping the trail back and forth in front of his feet with it. He was alert but not action-ready. That was his first mistake.

The men that came around the curve next were even less on top of things than the point man was. Their weapons were slung carelessly over their shoulders, not even seconds from firing position. The only contact they expected was with a half-dead pilot lying facedown on the trail, crawling like a wounded lizard. They flashed their lights into the brush bordering the trail with little enthusiasm and even less efficiency. They were relying on the point man to come up with their quarry.

Beeker waited until there were four of them on his side of the rock. When the rear man stepped passed Beeker's face, he pulled the vine in his left hand. Down the trail, a white shirt wrapped around a rock moved along the ground into the bushes. The point man caught the movement in his flash beam and let out a shout. Beeker then yanked the vine he held in his right hand, pulling the trip wire into place.

The point man hit the vine on the run. His right foot stopped dead at the ankle while his torso kept moving forward. His leg went rigid as the knee refused to bend in the wrong direction, and he went over forward, arms flailing and equipment flying. The second man went through the exact same dance routine and came down on top of the point man. The two of them plunged through the leaf-covered top of the tiger trap, bodies twisting and hands clawing at each other for support. The third man had the presence of mind to hop over the trip wire, but couldn't stop himself from falling headlong into the tiger trap. The fourth man stopped short in his tracks and stood dumbly, looking at the exposed pit, not saying or doing anything. Beeker leaped up behind him and opened the man's throat with his Sting. He hit the ground with a blood-wet, gurgling exhalation of breath, and didn't move. Scratch one.

In the tiger trap two men were still alive. The point man was out of the picture, impaled clean through on the bamboo stakes from the additional impact of his two comrades. Scratch two. The second man lay facedown on top of the point man's corpse, a stake poking through the fleshy part of his right thigh and another one sticking out the back of his right hand. He was dazedly convulsing, trying to tear his hand free. He was only making it worse. Blood was leaking out of his hand and dripping down between his fingers. The third man was on his back, splayed diagonally across the other living man's legs. He didn't look spiked anywhere but seemed hooked to the bamboo by the back of his web belt. He was trying to right himself in a panic, like a flipped-over turtle that knew a predator was near. He whimpered when he saw Beeker's black silhouette looking down on him and groped wildly for his weapon.

Beeker dropped into the pit, avoiding the spikes and straddling the two men. They stopped struggling and looked up at him, eyes wide and faces slick with sweat. Without hesitating, Beeker finished both of them with his knife. They died quickly and quietly, blood spurting around Beeker's wrist. He took no satisfaction in the task, and felt no guilt, either. It was just something to be done, and he did it. Without dwelling on the matter, he wiped himself and his knife on the top man's fatigues, relieved the three corpses of their weapons and web belts, and climbed out of the pit. Cowboy, Boone, and Applebaum were waiting for him.

"Put all the bodies in and then cover it over," he ordered them.

While his men carried the three rear-column troopers to their grave, Beeker conducted a weapons check by flashlight. They now had six M-16s and one M-60, with twelve spare thirty-round magazines for the '16s and two one-hundred-round disintegrating metal belts for the '60. The commandos carried no sidearms, but that was okay. The weapons were only in fair condition—they needed cleaning badly. Beeker knew from experience that dirty M-16s had the annoying habit of jamming at inopportune moments, so they'd have to deal with that soon.

The tiger trap was now fully covered and, with the addition of some brush scattered over it, had rejoined the contour of the trail. It was all but invisible to the untrained eye. His men awaited further orders. Distributing the weapons among them—Applebaum, of course, took charge of the '60 while the rest shouldered two M-16s apiece—Beeker took one last visual check of the area, then led his men up the trail toward the altiplano.

They stopped where they had stopped before, where the trail broke out of the jungle. Beeker scanned the sky for the helicopters and sighted all five of them in widely scattered positions, crisscrossing the river for several hundred yards up- and downstream. If he and his men moved quickly and carefully up the trail, they should be able to make it to the altiplano without being spotted. Once there they had to reach the next area of cover, but since the Peruvians weren't expecting a half-dead pilot to make it that far, they probably wouldn't be looking up there. Beeker figured they were safe as long as they had the darkness to cover them.

He was right. They found the camp, Harry and Jackie packed and waiting, with only a minimum of difficulty. Dawn was beginning to lighten the deep blue of the eastern sky, and while Beeker knew they could all stand a good rest, he also knew that they had to get the hell out of the area fast. Fifteen minutes, maybe, they could spare. Ten of them to clean and strip the weapons, the other five for a breather. Then they had to move.

"Any unusual activity on the road?" Beeker asked Harry while they were scouring the muzzle ends of their M-16 barrels with toothbrushes. As Harry knew, he was refer- ring to military vehicles.

"Not that I noticed. Seems clear," he replied, flipping the assembly over to clear the chamber of its thick patches of carbonization. Without any cleaning solution on hand, they had to rely strictly on elbow grease to scour the weapon down to its chrome-plated bore. They wouldn't have time to do a very thorough job, but it would be good enough for a minimum amount of firing. Beeker hoped even a minimum would be unnecessary, but he knew they had to be prepared for it.

On Beeker's orders, all the weapons were reassembled, without benefit of lubrication. It was his experience that '16s fired well enough cold to forego lubing for long periods of time; in fact, he'd seen more of the rifles screwed up by too much gun oil attracting crud than from forgetting to grease them up. Again, minimum maintenance had to be sufficient.

Finally, after stowing the weapons out of sight in the two Land-Rovers, they headed north on the road away from there. It was just before seven, and the sun was pushing itself clear of the mountain peaks in the east. There was no sign of military activity either on the road or in the air above them. Beeker, sitting in the shotgun seat next to Rosie in the lead Rover, scanned the sky nervously. It looked like they were getting away before a general alarm could be sounded. Ignoring the feeling of impending doom clutching at his stomach, Beeker

115

studied the maps. They had many hours of riding ahead of them. He hoped their luck would hold out. But now they were ready if it didn't. He felt a bit better—but not much.

# 9

There were nine of them, and they looked more like gangsters than freedom fighters. Beeker's first thought was that they'd armed themselves at a PLO rummage sale. Five of them carried Chinese-made AK-47s, scuffed wooden stocks under their armpits, crooked banana clips protruding comically. There was also a heavily taped-up M-16, two dusty Belgian FN/FALs, and what looked like a museum-piece German Schmeisser MP-4O machine pistol. If they could get off a dozen clean rounds between them, it would be a miracle. Beeker tried not to laugh in their faces.

The six of them had arrived at the designated rendezvous point a half-hour earlier, after bouncing along all day on the winding, two-lane "highway." They'd encountered no police or army patrols, though they'd heard the sounds of distant chopper blades often enough to make them nervous. But the beautiful scenery they drove through had a calming effect on all their nerves. The road they were taking passed through a couple of other small, Chinchero-sized towns before dropping down into the Vilcanota River Valley. A rickety old wooden bridge took them across the river, and then the road turned sharper northward, paralleling the waterway's plunge toward the swift-flowing Urubamba River and ultimately the Amazon. Beeker dozed fitfully and took over the driving from Rosie a bit north of the monumental ruins of Machu Picchu, an ancient city clinging to a mountaintop across the river.

They reached the city of Chaullay in later afternoon, the rain hitting them just as they crossed the magnificent Choquechaca Bridge—portal to the great Vilcabamba mountain range. Their destination was only a few miles ahead. From there they'd be taken to Guiterrez, and then they could get this lousy business over with.

The rendezvous point was a flat open area, the dead end of a mountain road halfway up the mountain. There was no one in sight when they pulled the Land-Rovers in and parked them next to each other in the middle of the clearing. But the tickle on the back of Beeker's neck told him people were there, whether he saw anyone or not.

Leaving their weapons under wraps, the five Black Berets arranged themselves in and around the Land-Rovers so that every angle of approach was covered. Jackie, thankfully, was in a dead-to-the-world snooze, as she had been for most of the day's traveling. Beeker made no move to wake her.

Things remained quiet for thirty minutes while they waited patiently. Then the nine armed men appeared at the edge of the clearing, and Beeker knew the wait was over. He let them make the first move.

The little guy with the Schmeisser strolled forward. Beeker figured he was the leader from the arrogance of his walk. He had close-cropped Brillo-like hair, coffee-colored skin, and aviator specs with lenses tinted a brownish yellow. His shirt was a garishly patterned, shiny polyester thing unbuttoned to his stomach. A gold cross sat on his hairless chest. His pants were baggy, double-knit brown bell-bottoms, and his Nike running shoes were brand-new. His smile was wide and insincere.

"Hello, hello, hello," he said jovially, with a slight Spanish accent. He came to a stop fifteen feet away from the Land-Rovers. "My name is Colonel Morales." Looking at Jackie asleep in the back of one of the Rovers, he said, "And this is Miss Simmons, I would guess. We are all *very* happy to see you." Jackie stirred sluggishly and raised her head. Beeker gave the guy his Cherokee stone face.

"I'm Beeker," he said. "You're here to take us to Guiterrez. Roll back the artillery."

Morales grinned apologetically and dropped his chin onto his chest. Jackie sat up and rubbed her eyes. None of the eight men pointing their automatic weapons at them moved.

"You'll have to forgive our rudeness, Mr. Beeker, but we have to be *very* careful these days. The Army has put a very big price on all of our heads, and many men have tried to collect it. It is not meant as anything personal against you, you understand." He stopped talking and the stupid grin returned to his face.

Beeker shrugged. "AKs pointing at my face make me nervous. A strange quirk I developed in Vietnam. There's no telling what I might do."

Colonel Morales's grin faded a little bit. "I understand perfectly, Mr. Beeker. I am much the same way about men I have not yet searched for weapons."

So it was going to be like that, a showdown. Beeker pushed himself off the Rover's hood he was leaning against, but kept his hands in his pockets. His men were tensed and ready, waiting for a signal from their leader. Morales's boys surrounding them were nervously fingering their rifles, eager to shoot and make some noise. It had probably been hours since they'd had any fun. Morales's right fist clenched and unclenched around the Schmeisser's black pistol grip. Beeker turned and faced him directly but said nothing. It was a standoff, and he felt like Gary Cooper.

After a good half-minute of this, Morales barked a quick

119

order to his men without unlocking his eyes from Beeker's. The eight all eagerly jerked their weapons into the under-the-arm spray position and waited. Looked like fun was on the way.

At last Morales said, "You will all please come away from the Jeeps, walking slowly with your hands in the air. Keep walking until I tell you to stop."

Beeker shook his head. "I'm sorry, Colonel, but I just can't do that." He paused dramatically and said, "Applebaum?"

Marty, sitting in one of the Rovers' shotgun seats, brought up the M-60 he'd been patiently holding in his lap. He trained it at Morales's thyroid gland, grinning and chewing slowly on some gum. A murmur went through Morales's men, but nobody moved.

"That's an M-60, Colonel, in case you can't quite see it. And it'll chop your body in half before your boys here can even fire their peashooters."

"Beeker, what the *hell* are you doing?" Jackie was obviously awake now, and intent on injecting herself into the proceedings. "These people are our *friends*, and we're here to *help* them, not make them angry!" She stood up in the Land-Rover and, without even noticing, became the focal point for eight itchy automatic weapons. She made a lunge for Applebaum, but Harry grabbed her by the back of her shirt and pulled her back down into her seat. She started to protest, but the Greek's big hairy hand muzzled her public address system.

"You should listen to the beautiful lady, Mr. Beeker," Morales said with exaggerated regret. "She knows what she is talking about. We have no interest in seeing any of you hurt. We are simply protecting ourselves. You must understand that." He raised his left hand in a gesture of friendly futility.

"I do," Beeker answered. "Which is why I can't let

120

you take our weapons. My job here is to protect Ms. Simmons, and I can't do that without weapons."

"Yes, but you no longer *need* any weapons. You are safely in our hands, and we are responsible for your well-being from this moment on."

"Thanks, but no thanks, Colonel. I make it a policy never to give up my weapon. You just take us along to see Mr. Guiterrez, and if everything's jake, we'll become the best of friends. Right now, I'll stick with my insurance policy here."

Morales paused and chewed his lower lip. Applebaum's M-60 didn't move from its mark.

"The *Jefe* is not going to like this," Morales said, shaking his head.

"Tough shit on the *Jefe*, Colonel. He invited us here, and we come only on our own terms. Take it, or we turn around and head back to Cusco." It was a ridiculous idea, but Morales didn't know that. Beeker let him chew on that for a while. He chewed for about fifteen seconds.

"As you wish, Señor Beeker. You leave me no choice, eh? But I guess you know that. You may keep your weapons for the time being. The *Generál* will decide what to do when we reach camp. *Vámanos!*" Morales tried to appear philosophical about the whole thing, but he was plainly unnerved. Beeker's suspicious itch got worse.

On Beeker's orders, the six of them donned their packs and shouldered their weapons, and then stashed the Land-Rovers for later use. They left the two vehicles, covered over with brush, in a spot about fifty yards below the clearing. Beeker hoped the things'd still be there when they needed them later, but a strong feeling told him Morales planned to dispose of them as soon as the party was safely in Guiterrez's hands. These people obviously wanted Jackie and the Black Berets totally dependent on them. He vowed not to let that happen. Keeping their weapons was the first big step.

The combined group of fifteen fanned out onto a circum-mountain trail in a loose, tourist-patrol style. Two skinny, long-haired teenagers with the PRC AKs took the point about thirty yards forward. Two toothless old guys with the FNs took the rear, chewing and spitting a lot. The remaining Kalashnikovs spread wide, while the M-16-in-traction fastened himself, with obvious admiration, to Applebaum's M-60. From the look in the man's eyes, he believed the tough-looking machine gun was the *man's* weapon he so richly deserved graduation to. Applebaum ate the attention up.

A few yards in front of the strutting Applebaum and the silent Harry, Jackie was stumbling along sleepily. Beeker, Cowboy, and Rosie were all ahead of her by a few yards and pointedly ignoring her periodic whines. Morales, naturally, gravitated quickly to her side and tried lamely to chat her up. But Jackie was interested only in complaining; complaining about how tired she was, how the leather straps in her sandals were hurting her feet, how the pack with her clothes was too heavy for her to carry, how the altitude and high humidity were giving her a headache. Morales eventually gave up on conversation with her and let her moans go unnoticed. So she changed her tactics.

"How long do we have to walk before we get to General Guiterrez's camp?"

"A few days, no more," Morales said brightly, happy to deliver what he thought was good news. Jackie cursed indelicately.

"Why do we have to walk?" she asked him. "Isn't there any other easier way for us to get there?" She was thinking about the Land-Rovers they had left behind, which, her earlier complaints to the contrary, suddenly seemed like luxury limousines to her. Or maybe she was expecting burly natives to carry her on their backs in a pole-mounted chair?

Morales shook his little head sadly. "There are not many roads up here in the Vilcabamba—our meeting place back there was the closest a road comes to *La Fortaleza*. From there one must walk, or one must fly." Bullshit, Beeker thought, but said nothing. It was just another way for them to wear us down.

"Can't a helicopter come pick us up?" Beeker turned around to make sure Jackie was serious. She was. Next she'd want to hail a cab.

Morales employed his humbly apologetic face this time. "Unfortunately, no, Miss Simmons. We have a bare handful of helicopters that we use mostly for supply purposes. Fuel is quite precious and expensive. That is why we need the help of the great United States of America in our struggle—that is why we asked you to come."

Jackie didn't have an answer to that one, but a reminder of her noble mission puffed up her spirits a bit. Beeker snorted contemptuously at the line of bullshit Morales was dishing out. The guy sounded like he'd been memorizing the *Ronald Reagan Phrase Book of Idiot Politics*.

Conversation died. They tramped through the mountain greenery for another hour, until Morales called a halt and signaled for a camp. It was just past six o'clock—twilight here in the mountains where the sun takes a long time to disappear, but when it does, darkness and cold air move in swiftly.

Beeker let Morales and his men handle the outer perimeter while he grouped his own men around Jackie Simmons in the shelter of an evergreenlike tree. He assigned a rotating two-hour watch and portioned out the cold rations supplied by their guides. They ate in silence, after only a brief complaint from Jackie about the absence of hot food. The lack of a fire would be felt more later, Beeker knew, after the night air had moved in for its shift. Beeker made sure Jackie put on most of the clothes that were in her pack, then gathered a cushion of leaves for her to sleep on. He made sure she was comatose before leaving her, and sat down next to Rosie, who'd drawn first watch.

"Is this whole setup making you as nervous as it's making me?" Rosie asked after a while.

"And then some," Beeker said, nodding.

"Do you think we're smellin' something real, or just actin' like a bunch of homeboys?"

Beeker shrugged. "Hell—I wish I knew, Rosie. We'll just have to watch out, be ready, and find out when it happens, I guess. Whatever comes down, though, I'm sure we can handle it."

"Like shit's brown, m'man," Rosie answered, and slapped Beeker's outstretched palm. He paused nervously, and then spoke. "Billy . . . I got to apologize for that business before. Me and the Runt were out of line. It was bad business. I don't know what the fuck came over me. It ain't gonna happen again, at least not on this end. You got that?"

Beeker could see Boone's eyes in the night, burning into his. He knew what it was that had come over his friend before, and more, what stronger force had taken over now. Roosevelt Boone smelled danger, and it was real close. Behind it, on a distant wind, was death. That had brought the fighting man back out in Rosie. Beeker reached out and touched his buddy's shoulder.

"It's history, Rosie," he said. It was enough. They sat together for a while longer, watching the stars through the tree covering. Then, without a word, Beeker got out his blanket, rolled himself into it, and went immediately to sleep.

\*     \*     \*

Their march continued through two more full days and half of the third. The faintly marked trail took them deeper into the Vilcabamba, up steep slopes of scrubby, high-altitude grass, and back down into forested river valleys. They saw no one in these hills, though they occasionally noticed terraced farms clinging to hillsides on other valley slopes. Nor did they hear any helicopters patrolling or other aircraft flying over. They were alone up here. It was as if they had stepped into another world or had been transported back in time, before the *conquistadores*, before the Incas, before civilization. It was as if they had these mountains to themselves.

But close to noon on the third day of traveling with Morales and his men, Beeker began feeling that tickle on his neck. They were close, he knew. Eyes were watching them. Gunsights were following them. Fully an hour later they crested a high ridge connecting two treeless mountain peaks, and they were there.

Morales halted, smiled, and, with a flourish, performed a sweeping toreadorlike gesture with his arm. It made Beeker think of Ricardo Montalban pointing at a Chrysler.

"*La Fortaleza*, gentlemen and lady," he announced with pride. "Our fortress in the mountains, from where our people's revolution will be launched." Missing only was a long drumroll and rousing trumpet fanfare.

Bullshit aside, the place was impressive. A verdant river valley was unrolled like a lush carpet before them. All around, towering mountains rose like angry spirits from the earth, trying desperately to break free of their rock-bound prison. A dense green canopy of evergreenlike *chachacomo* trees draped the hollow of the valley, sheltered like Shangri-La from the outside world by a dome of perpetual fog and snowcapped fortress walls. It looked wild, innocent, and uninhabited, and would no doubt go

125

completely unnoticed from the air—unless someone knew it was there.

From their vantage point on the ridge, they could just begin to see through the protective forest canopy to the armed camp that was hidden below. It was like looking at an anthill and suddenly discovering that it swarmed with thousands and thousands of ants. Beeker couldn't tell how many thousands of people were swarming in this mountain retreat, but there were lots of them, that was for sure. Men and women were everywhere, some in military fatigues, some in colorful *nativo* dress, and some in duds straight off the rack at Sears. There were wooden cabins built on stilts, tents, leafy lean-tos, ancient stone warehouses, and active cave entrances, all connected by wide, well-trod paths. And there were weapons everywhere. Assault rifles slung over shoulders, hip-holstered police revolvers and army-issue automatics, and what appeared to be Soviet-made ZU-23 anti-aircraft guns, their wheels trenched and firing areas sandbagged. Beeker was stunned. This was no ragtag, haphazardly equipped rebel horde—it was a well-outfitted army. What kind of help did these guys need? Who were they trying to fool? And why?

"It keeps gettin' worse, Billy." Rosie was next to him, shaking his head and nervously fingering his M-16. "One more unpleasant surprise, and I'm gonna shit, I swear. I've *had* it."

Beeker laughed, but he felt chilled. Turning to the woman, he said, "Well, Jackie. What do you make of this? Still think these gallant, freedom-loving unfortunates are in need of our help?" He was needling her. Normally, he didn't like pulling this sort of I-told-you-so bullshit on *anybody*, but Jackie deserved it.

She didn't answer for a few moments and just looked at the camp with uncomprehending confusion. Then she looked at Beeker. The expression on her face was pathetic. Beeker turned away and followed Morales into the camp.

The escort party led them to their accommodations—a renovated cave on the camp's western edge. It wasn't the Ritz, but for a cave it wasn't bad. A string of light bulbs trailed across the rock ceiling, filling the furnished cavern with a harsh, unshaded light. Handwoven blankets hung from hemp ropes, providing rudimentary room divisions. The scattered furniture was a mixture of rickety, yard-sale castoffs, hand-rigged wood-and-rope constructions, and Flintstone-like hand-hewn built-ins. Morales showed them around, like an eager bellboy, and then turned to leave.

"And the *Generál* has arranged for Miss Simmons to stay in our main headquarters building."

Jackie brightened at that, but Beeker stepped in.

"Forget it, Colonel—she stays here with us. Like I told you before, Ms. Simmons's safety is our responsibility, so there will always be at least one of us with her. And she sleeps *here* with us."

Jackie didn't like it nearly as much as Morales didn't like it. She said sarcastically, "And I suppose you boys are going to wipe my ass for me as well?"

Before Applebaum could step forward and volunteer for the job, Beeker said, "I'm getting tired of telling you this, Jackie, but I've got a job to do, and I'm going to do it—whether you, Morales, or Guiterrez likes it or not. So if I say you wear us like a pair of soiled panties, then that's the way it is—no argument." He turned his attention to Morales and told him, "Now go tell Guiterrez that we'll see him as soon as he'd like, after we've cleaned up." Morales shrugged and was gone.

Beeker and Rosie gave the joint a quick once over and sent Jackie to use the shower someone had rigged up by the back wall. It was a cleverly done rope-pull operation, with an electrically warmed overhead cistern and a gravel-covered drain. To give her some modicum of privacy, the five men removed themselves from the room and sat out by the fitted-stone cave entrance. They lazed indolently in the dirt, weapons invisible but within easy reach, and surveyed the camp.

"Looks like the way we came in is the only exit to this valley," Rosie said to no one in particular.

Beeker answered him, "I doubt it, both for Guiterrez's sake and for ours. I don't think he's dumb enough to lock himself in a valley with only one way out. Cowboy— you've got the most innocent face here—why don't you take a stroll to look for the latrine and see if you can spot more of the setup." The pilot nodded and moved off, whistling like an altar boy on his way home from church.

"You know what this place reminds me of?" Rosie had an inwardly searching look in his eyes, mixed with a sort of fearful nostalgia. It was a look almost all Vietnam vets got in their eyes when something forcefully reminded them of a painful memory they'd be better off forgetting. None of the others answered him. It would be something he'd have to speak aloud for himself, like an exorcism ritual.

"You remember that NVA base camp I was held in, a few miles off Highway 9, near Sepone?"

They all did. It was not something easily forgotten. It had been early 1971, the beginning of the rainy season, and Rosie had gotten himself caught while on a recon mission deep into Laos. The company of NVA regulars he had stumbled onto killed all his indigenous team members and then took him back—lashed upside-down to a pole, like an animal—to their operations center for interrogation. There Rosie was mercilessly tortured for hours by a ruthless NVA colonel and probably would've died if Beeker, Marty, Harry, and Cowboy hadn't slipped into the OC later that night and snatched him out from under their noses—blowing the place all to hell on the way out.

Guiterrez's fortress did indeed resemble that Operations Center. It had been built completely into the side of a hollowed-out mountain and covered over with a jungle-heavy camouflage net. Its caving system had been incredible—hand-dug caverns big enough to hold a half-dozen six-by trucks; several military equipment factories, mostly for repacking artillery shells; a two-hundred-bed field hospital; a communications and command center; and billeting for two batallions of NVA regulars. It was an astounding bit of work, all of it done completely under cover and kept that way for who knew how long. Beeker had called in the B-52s after they'd gotten the hell gone, and the arc light from the air strike had been visible twenty miles away, across the border into Vietnam.

They all silently relived that night together. The taste of the jungle-river water that covered their entry and retreat; the bitter smell of Applebaum's satchel charges; and the long walk home. It was there, almost real—*too* real.

Rosie broke the spell. "It was number ten, man—the worst night of my fucking life." Suddenly, he laughed harshly. "And here I am again. I must be fucking *crazy.*"

"No more than the rest of us, Rosie," Harry put in. There was unspoken agreement. There was something about an insanity shared with others that made it seem just a bit more sane.

An approaching commotion drew their attention. It was Morales leading a group of armed men, a larger group than before. He seemed perturbed. With them—surrounded by them, actually—was Cowboy, who was being urged to walk faster than he wanted to. His face now read like the altar boy who'd been caught peeking into the girl's locker room.

"Mr. Beeker," Morales began, trying hard to maintain a masquerade of civility, "you will please not interfere with our security perimeter. You and your men *must* respect our need to maintain camp security and should therefore restrict your movements to your quarters. To go anywhere else is forbidden—unless you have permission and an escort.''

Cowboy, meanwhile, loudly proclaimed the innocence of his activity. ''Shit, man, I was only looking for the damn latrine! Can't a man even take a leak around here without an armed guard?'' Morales ignored his protests while his men stood around brandishing their weapons, trying to look tough.

''Look, Morales,'' Beeker said, stepping forward. ''We don't like being here any more than you like having us. We're trying to be nice guys about this, but restricting us to our cave here isn't going to help our attitudes any. You just give us a little room and we'll behave ourselves. Unless, of course, you give us reason to do otherwise. Do I make myself clear?''

Morales's nostrils flared in anger; his Schmeisser chafed at the bit. A wave of muttering went through his men, and they slowly spread themselves in a semicircle around the cave entrance. Behind him, Beeker's men edged closer to their weapons. Tension filled the air like smoke.

Suddenly, Morales's expression changed. A near-smile came to his lips, and his eyes flickered to something over Beeker's shoulder.

''I don't think you are in any position to make demands, Señor Beeker,'' he said smugly.

Beeker heard a rustle from the cave entrance behind him and then a muttered curse from one of his men. Something was wrong. He turned his head slowly, keeping one eye on Morales.

Jackie was standing there, hair pasted to her head, a soaked-through T-shirt stretched over her to mid-thigh. She was shivering, but it wasn't because she was cold. A

130

man was standing behind her, one hand clamping her elbows back, the other holding a K-bar knife to her throat. He had a mustache and a space between his two front teeth. He was smiling crookedly.

"Good to know our li'l cave has a back door, eh, Sarge?" Cowboy said with self-recrimination in his voice. "What a stupid bunch of turkeys *we* are." Beeker didn't say anything, but he certainly agreed. He should have made a more thorough check.

"Now that we have this unpleasant business all straightened out, you will leave your weapons and come with me. General Guiterrez is *most* anxious to meet with you." He motioned to his men and turned to go.

But it was far from over. As soon as Morales's back was turned and his men had dropped their pose of readiness, the Black Berets moved into action. Beeker gave a quick, covert signal to Harry—the closest to Jackie—then took a two-step leap onto Morales's back. The man went down under him with a yelp of surprise.

Harry's right foot rose in a wide arc and kicked the knife away from Jackie's throat. The man recoiled in surprise, taking a step backward and letting Jackie's arms go. She dropped like a bag of wet laundry. Before the man could recover, Harry delivered a crippling one-two combo—a chop to the throat with the outer edge of his right hand and a savage thrust to the nose with the heel of his left palm. The man screamed, and his face erupted with red liquid like a burst blood-filled balloon. Meanwhile Applebaum had rolled Jackie into the cave entrance and came up with his M-60. Rosie and Cowboy had likewise dived for their weapons. The freedom fighters scattered, looking for the nearest cover.

Morales struggled fiercely in Beeker's grip. He had fallen on his Schmeisser and was desperately trying to pull it out from under his chest. Beeker used his weight to make sure he couldn't. He took a handful of the man's short hair and yanked back as far as the neck could go. That brought forth a torrent of Spanish obscenities and a downshift in the struggling. The feather-light Sting was now in Beeker's right hand, and then it was pressing into Morales's throat.

"*Freeze*—unless you're looking for a new air hole, motherfucker," Beeker said quietly through his teeth. Morales ceased all movement immediately.

"Okay, cunt-breath, listen *carefully* to what I say. If you don't do *exactly* what I tell you, I'm going to ventilate your neck. Got that?" He pulled a little harder on the hair and sliced off some skin for emphasis. Morales's eyes bulged, and his head bounced a panicky affirmative.

"Good. Now we're going to roll over onto your left-hand side—very, *very* slowly—and you're going to move the Schmeisser in a very slow line until it gets to your mouth. You will not *once* let the muzzle leave your skin. If I see *any* daylight between the weapon and your chest, I'm gonna open you up like a catfish ready for frying. And when that barrel touches your lips, I want you to suck on it like it was your mama's tit. Now *do it*!"

He did it. He tipped over onto his left arm, effectively putting his body between Beeker and his trigger-itchy men, and guided the black metal barrel of the MP-40 through the beads of sweat on his chest. When it reached his mouth, he put it in only to his clenched teeth. Beeker flicked the knife to indicate his disapproval.

"Gobble that thing, shit-face! I want to see it *all the way* into your filthy mouth, or I'll break your teeth with the sight!"

Obediently, Morales opened his mouth wide enough to admit the cylindrical sight that sat on top of the barrel, just behind the muzzle. He pushed the black steel tube farther back toward his throat, stopping only when he gagged. After closing his lips around it, the man shot Beeker a look of pure hate.

"Very *good*, Colonel," Beeker said, using the man's rank like an insult. "You suck on that like a pro! I bet you've done this sort of thing before." The extra humiliation was unnecessary—and maybe dangerous—but Beeker couldn't resist. He'd been bottled up for too long. He continued with his instructions: "Now we're gonna get up on our feet, Colonel—very, *very* slowly—and back up into the cave. Let's hope none of your boys out there try any bush-league heroics, 'cause if any of 'em *do*, you'll be a bag of *cold meat* before you can even *pray*! Are you still with me?"

Morales nodded briskly, breathing with difficulty through his nose. His eyes held Beeker's, broadcasting trapped-animal hostility. Beeker only smiled indulgently and signaled his captive to rise. They got to their feet in unison, and Beeker tried as best he could to shield himself with the smaller man's body. With any luck, they'd be inside the cave before one of Morales's better marksman could try his luck.

"Cover me," Beeker called out to his men, and started pulling at Morales's hair to get him moving. He responded like a trained dog on a leash, and within seconds they were both safely inside. Morales was instantly disarmed and dropped to the ground, rendering him harmless and out of their way.

"Well, Sarge, what in fuck's name do we do now?" Cowboy wanted to know.

Beeker took stock. Out front, Morales's men still showed confusion. They were keeping to cover but obviously didn't know whether they should back off, storm the cave, shoot

133

in a gas grenade, or call for an executive-level decision. In their position, Beeker probably would've opted for a combination of the gas and storming approaches, but, like good robot soldiers, these guys chose the last alternative: Never make any decision that you can pass on to someone of higher rank. They hunkered down and called for the boss. Beeker was glad these guys were merely soldiers and not Marines. Their unwillingness to take initiative would give him time to think.

But Morales distracted him. "You are all dead men," he told them.

Rosie laughed at him. "Forget it, pal. That's like tellin' a blind man you're gonna shut out the lights. We've been *dead men* for longer than you've been a *man*—so you'll have to do better than that pussy-shit jive." They all laughed at that, and the tension and fear that had gripped them seconds before was gone.

Then Applebaum called out, "Here comes the head man," and then all turned to check out the Big Chief.

The figure approaching with a strong, determined stride, was undoubtedly the head honcho. The way his men fanned out behind him, like the waves in a speedboat's wake, was a dead giveaway from a distance. Close up, his quiet regality pegged him instantly. It was as though he stood perpetually in a spotlight. He wore no insignia of rank on his neatly pressed uniform of green fatigues, but he didn't have to. No confirmation of his rank was needed. You just knew he was a general.

He was a handsome man, as well. Dark and fine-featured, he could've been a movie star. His unmistakable personal magnetism and charisma blazed like a Jack Kennedy or a Che Guevara. He had Castro's commanding presence but none of his boorishness. He had Reagan's sense of easygoing good humor but John Wayne's aura of strength and purpose. He was all things to all men; in short, the ultimate politician. Beeker had no doubt that he was on his way to becoming his country's next president.

Clearly, his men worshiped him.

Beeker didn't trust him farther than he could piss.

# 10

---

General Ramón Guiterrez came to a stop about thirty feet in front of the cave entrance and spread his arms wide from his body. His men hung back another thirty feet behind him, hesitant. He seemed unafraid and completely confident of his control of the situation. Beeker eyed him warily.

"Mr. Beeker, is it not?" He called out in unaccented English.

"That's right."

"I'd like to talk with you. As you can see, I am without weapons."

"No, I can't see. Strip, and I'll know for sure."

Guiterrez laughed heartily. "Morales told me you were a hard man, Mr. Beeker, and indeed you are." He shrugged philosophically. "But, if it will make you feel better . . ." He reached for the top button of his fatigue shirt.

"That won't be necessary, General. *I* trust you," Jackie said as she stepped past Beeker's angrily grasping hand into the light. *Damn* that woman. She had pulled on a pair of rumpled, baggy fatigue pants to complement her dirt-smeared T-shirt, but from the look on Guiterrez's face, her sex appeal was still quite evident. He smiled and bowed gallantly.

"Ah, Miss Simmons. It is indeed a pleasure to welcome you here." If he kisses her hand, Beeker thought, I'm gonna puke. He didn't. He kissed her on both cheeks. She loved it.

Next to him, Rosie said, "Billy, what do you say we leave the bitch here with her heroic buddies and just take our butts home? I'm *damn* tired of her."

"You and me both, Rosie—I'm tempted, believe me. But we've got to finish this job as agreed, even if our employer does her best to screw us up. Just as long as she doesn't get us all greased—"

"Yeah, and if we happen to fall by the wayside somewhere, I'll bet she ain't gonna lose any sleep over it—just so long as *her* skin don't get scratched, and her story gets on the tube."

The rest of them grunted their agreement and waited for the little tête-á-tête going on out there to conclude. Applebaum—who was sitting on top of Morales's back, knees holding the colonel's arms down, M-60 poked in the man's right ear—wanted to know what was going on. Jackie's sudden return provided the answer.

"The General's invited me to lunch," she said casually, as though she was getting ready to head out to the Burger King.

Rosie snorted and said, "Great. Is he sending out for Chinese food or whipping us up something all by his little self?"

She put her hands on her hips and looked at him crossly. "You needn't be so goddamn sarcastic," she informed him, like a mother telling an adolescent how to behave. "Just because some of his men are a little overzealous, you have no right to condemn him. He apologized. He explained. He has no intention of seeing any of us harmed, and if you think different, you're just too paranoid." She looked at their expressions of disbelief. "I trust him, even if none of you do."

"Hey," Applebaum called. "Before you guys take a

vote on whether to trust hotshot out there, maybe somebody should tell me what to do with this clown under me."

"Keep him as a hostage until Jackie comes back from lunch," Rosie suggested.

"That's a possibility," Beeker said, "but it would divide our energies and keep things tense around here. I'd like to avoid that if I can." His attention was diverted by some activity out front. After conferring briefly with his men, Guiterrez had turned back toward the cave. He was walking slowly in their direction. His men were, grudgingly, shouldering their weapons and leaving the scene.

"Mr. Beeker," came Guiterrez's oil-smooth voice. "I've ordered my men to withdraw. You should in no way feel threatened or in any danger. I now ask you to release Colonel Morales, and please accept my invitation to accompany Miss Simmons to lunch with me."

Beeker mulled it over. Either way open to him, he was giving something up. Giving up his edge if he turned Morales loose, giving up freedom of movement if he kept him. He didn't much fancy hunkering down in this cave with every weapon in the valley trained on them. . . .

"You've proved your point, Mr. Beeker," Guiterrez continued. "You may keep your weapons for the time being, even though it makes my men nervous. They think I am crazy to do this—they want to blast you out of that cave." He stopped there to let the implication sink in: I could easily change my mind, *gringo*, he was saying.

"Let short-stuff go," Beeker said to Marty. The ruffled man scrambled to his feet after Applebaum had rolled off him, and grabbed his Schmeisser from Harry—who'd removed the long, rectangular magazine before handing it to him. He exited the cave without a word, though his face said, "We'll even the score later, *chancho*." He and Guiterrez exchanged some inaudible Spanish, and then the colonel strode off, still pissed off but apparently mollified by something Guiterrez had told him—like maybe, "He's yours when this is over, *muchacho*."

"One thing, General," Beeker called out.

"And what is that?"

"We make that lunch a foursome."

"As you wish." He shrugged agreeably. "Shall we go?"

Jackie ran frantically for the water basin.

"Give us five or ten," Beeker said, glancing at her. "The Contessa has to put on her face."

Guiterrez laughed chumily. What a charmer.


On their way to lunch, Beeker asked Cowboy about the setup, without once taking his eyes from Guiterrez and Jackie. The two were getting along famously about twenty feet in front of them.

"Looks like we came in the main entrance," he began in a soft voice. "That appears to offer the quickest and easiest way out. I saw two other trails up the hills and out on either side, but they're both tough—they're steep inclines. There are also several caves farther toward the back there that look like they might lead out, but they appear heavily trafficked and guarded.

"Let me tell you the interesting part, though. I got as far as the back end of the valley there, and it dog-legs over to the southwest. I only got a quick look before they grabbed me, but I could tell somethin's going on there—and they *definitely* didn't want me to see it."

"What kind of something?"

"I don't really know. There's some long, thatched-roof buildings under camo-netting, and smoke comin' from their chimneys. And a funny smell in the air, too."

"Bomb factory, probably," Beeker offered.

Cowboy shook his head. "I don't know. That one's the

least interesting possiblity, and the one that doesn't fit, really. They were *real* unhappy about my being there—that's when I got grabbed and pushed back to the cave—but they didn't give much of a shit two minutes earlier when I toddled past their regular ammo stores. Can you figure it?''

Beeker grunted. No, he couldn't figure it, and he added the information to the growing store of uncertainties crowding his head. Join the gang, bub.


The Executive Dining Room was in the camp's main headquarters building, a stone-and-wood ranch house in the sheltered back end of the valley. It also housed the general's living quarters, and the operations and communications centers—a well-outfitted, comfortable setup.

The food was pretty good, too—raw trout marinated in a lemon and chili-pepper sauce, with a cold vegetable and potato stew on the side. It was a leisurely lunch, served by white-jacketed stewards who were in no hurry. Guiterrez and Jackie chatted loudly the entire time, mostly congratulating each other on how wonderful they each were. Morales sat silently, a bandage on his neck where Beeker had sliced him, and stared sullenly at his food. Beeker and Cowboy ate well but lightly, their weapons out of sight under the table but within quick reach.

When it was over, Guiterrez sat back with a sigh and wiped his mouth with his napkin. Very genteel. In fact, most of the general's manners indicated a monied, patrician upbringing. Beeker guessed a European finishing school and then an American university—Ivy League, probably. More information that didn't jibe: Why should this product of the very privileged upper class lead a so-called populist revolution? Certainly not for his deep-felt concern for the downtrodden lower classes. No way. The only thing that made sense to Beeker was that his family had been disenfranchized by the military coup—or perhaps even earlier, by the previous social-democratic regime. Was he now leading the struggle to restore the old guard back to their hilltop mansions? Was this "Let's clean out the corrupt military and all their co-conspirators" story a cover for that?

"May I assume that all of you are most anxious to see what I asked her here to see?" Guiterrez asked after a while, between sips on his cup of coffee.

"You may," Beeker answered him. That brought a smile from the general.

"Ever the blunt and forceful man, eh, Mr. Beeker?"

Billy didn't answer. He sat in a position of readiness, waiting for Guiterrez to continue.

The general said, "Why don't we adjourn to the conference room where we'll be much more comfortable?" He got up from his chair, helped by a steward who pulled the thing back from behind him.

They followed him into an adjoining room, a darker one, with four chairs arranged in a semicircle facing a portable movie screen. Morales shut the door behind them and took his place behind a threaded-to-roll 16mm movie projector. Guiterrez poured a couple of brandies for himself and Jackie—Beeker and Cowboy both refused the offer—and lovingly, meticulously prepared a fat cigar for smoking. Only after relaxing in his brown leather chair and drawing several mouthfuls of smoke from his cigar did he finally begin telling them what this was all about. Or at least his side of it.

"The film I am about to show you is a collection of a number of things," he said. "There is some footage taken by men in my employ, showing meetings between a number of officials in government, business, organized crime, the police and the military, and the American espionage establishment here in Peru. They were all co-conspirators in the coup that toppled our last democratic government, and they are also the ones who are responsible for keeping the current one in office. Needless to say, they all profit enormously from the way the country is now run—from the exclusive access they have to our nation's legal and illegal businesses.

"The film will also show documentation to prove these allegations: records of huge Swiss bank accounts operated by all the officials you will see, exportation documents that cover for the millions of dollars' worth of cocaine that leave this country; evidence of the CIA's direct involvement in financing the group that first destabilized the economy under President Torio and then toppled him; copies of the sweetheart contracts signed immediately by the new government with certain multinational corporations involved in mining and agricultural activities here; and more.

"This is not at all a simple matter, and neither is it a pretty one. What we have here is the wholesale betrayal of an entire country to serve the rapacious greed of a few vicious men. They are bleeding my country dry, and they are flooding the world with a deadly and insidious drug!"

Cowboy coughed and barely stopped himself from smiling. Beeker thought he saw the welling of tears in the corners of Guiterrez's eyes. It was a stirring performance, but it was just that—a performance. Beeker didn't believe in the general's concern for his country any more now than he did before. The man was trying hard to convince them— and he was hiding his real motives. Beeker wondered if he'd ever get to the bottom of this, and whether he really wanted to. The truth was always uglier than people's fictionalized version.

"And what's in it for you, General?" Beeker poked at the guy a little, to see how he reacted.

"Well," he said with a candid grin, "if I were to say

that I would be satisfied just to see my country saved from these jackals, I'm afraid I'd be lying." He paused here to allow Beeker to fully appreciate the depths of his honesty. All he got was the stone face.

"At the risk of sounding immodest," he went on, "I think the country could benefit from my leadership talents. Once this present regime of carrion-eating animals is disposed of, I will play any role my people choose for me, in front or behind the scenes." He waved his manicured, cigar-holding hand magnanimously. "I am here to serve the greater good of the Peruvian republic."

"Who's bankrolling you, General?"

Guiterrez looked at Beeker. He didn't like that question. "I beg your pardon?" he asked.

"Where is the money to finance your revolution coming from? You're obviously well set-up here—ammunition, supplies, even luxuries for the commander. There's lots of money behind you, and I'm asking you where it's coming from. That should be a simple question to answer."

There was silence. Beeker always liked to know who was paying for things—revolutions, politicians, shopping centers, *anything*. That told you who expected to benefit the most, legally and illegally. Beeker wanted to know who was going to benefit from Guiterrez's revolution, which was being fought in the name of the Peruvian people. Certainly *they* weren't the ones keeping Guiterrez in brandy and his men in AKs.

Jackie came to the general's defense. "Beeker, I'm the reporter here, and I ask the questions. And the General's telling the story. He's *not* the story."

Beeker couldn't believe she was saying this to him. "You call yourself a reporter, and you tell me you're not interested in what's behind this operation? You've got to be pulling my leg!"

Jackie reddened a bit, and this time Guiterrez came to

143

her defense. "I appreciate your speaking for me, Miss Simmons, but you should know. If I am here asking for help from the people of the United States, I should be ready to tell them where the money for this revolution is coming from now. It is only fair." He turned his attention to Beeker and told him: "To be honest with you, our supplies right now come mostly from piracy—from what we can steal from our corrupt government in the way of weapons, ammunition, rations, etc. Money comes from various sources: business people; other governments in this area, who naturally would rather not be identified; and even some from the CIA, funneled through other organizations. I don't think they know at present that they are helping our cause. I hope that once our story is told in your country, and the outcry of the people is heard, your government will help us with what we need. I feel confident that once the truth is known, your people will no longer let their money—both public and private—go toward keeping these greedy pigs in power."

After all that, the film was almost an anticlimax. With Guiterrez providing play-by-play commentary, the rest of them watched a parade of smiling faces—some in uniform, and some in the charcoal-colored, three-piece tailored suits that are as much of a uniform for diplomats as fatigues are for military men—shaking hands a lot, exchanging documents, sitting around country estate patio tables talking to each other, getting in and out of helicopters, that sort of thing. Then there were pictures of the documents Guiterrez had referred to: bank statements; canceled checks; export licenses; bills of lading; contracts; etc. Then other, clandestinely shot footage of Peruvian Army regulars guarding jungle installations, one described by Guiterrez as a training camp for terrorists alleged to be far-left radicals, but actually government-controlled agents-provocateurs, and oth-

144

ers described as cocaine processing plants. The latter produced a sudden nudge from Cowboy at Beeker's elbow.

The film lasted about fifteen minutes. When it was over, Beeker found himself unconvinced. While he didn't really doubt any of the information—the sort of business depicted was standard operating procedure in this hemisphere— none of the so-called evidence was really iron-clad. You had to accept first what Guiterrez told you, and then everything fit together—but the other way around didn't work quite as well. The evidence was all circumstantial, explained only by the theory, explaining nothing much really by itself, except that the government seemed corrupt, and lots of these guys in government and business seemed awfully friendly. And who was to say this "evidence" was genuine—Guiterrez?

Beeker shrugged inwardly. Not his problem. He was only the baby-sitter on this trip, not the reporter. Digging behind and underneath this crap was Jackie's job; all he had to worry about was getting her and the tapes out of here intact. He would merely put his defenses onto a higher level of alert and push the rest of the stuff out of his mind. Guiterrez's credibility was Jackie's lookout, and if she was any good as a reporter, she'd check everything out before it even got *near* a national news show.

When the lights came up, Jackie was gushing all over herself. So much for her reporter's credentials, Beeker thought. Obviously, this was a sensational story as far as she was concerned, something to be rushed onto the air as soon as possible, to attract as much attention to herself as possible. It had been all neatly tied up and dropped into her eager little hands. Guiterrez couldn't have asked for a better patsy.

"General, that was *wonderful*," she said, practically licking her lips in anticipation. "I commend you on the diligence with which you prepared the film—it's model

145

reporting. My superiors at the Cable News Service will be delighted with it, I can assure you." Beeker could almost see her mentally cleaning away a spot for the awards this story was going to win her. Probably spending the money from her raise, too.

"I'm glad you approve, Miss Simmons." The guy was beaming shamelessly. "It took much hard work and the courage of many people, and I feel it was worth it."

Go ahead and smile, General, Beeker said to himself. Your fish is hooked. Reel her in.

On the way back to the cave, Cowboy could barely contain himself. He waited until the woman and the general were a good twenty paces in front of them, then he told Beeker in a quiet voice, "That cocaine processing plant in the film wasn't no government-run operation."

"Oh, no?"

"Yeah—it's right here in our backyard," he said, rolling his eyes in the direction of the valley's dog-leg, where earlier he'd run into trouble.

"No shit," Beeker said with a slow smile. "That does put things in an interesting light, doesn't it?" He scratched a spot on his right calf with the muzzle of his M-16. His trigger finger itched.

"What do you think's going on, Beek?" Cowboy's eyes casually roved the landscape, like an only moderately interested tourist.

"I don't know, but it stinks worse than a hog-hauler in August, that's for damn sure. No question now that this hole-kisser is trying to set us up for something—and Jackie's jumping in with both feet. If the film's bogus, then I'd guess he's just another disgruntled politician who's trying any way he can to get himself into power. If this film on

U.S. television can win him American logistic support, then he's in.''

"Funny thing is, though," Cowboy said, "that the information the film documents is probably correct. Everything I hear tells me the military government here *does* help float the coke trade—exports have skyrocketed since they took over.''

Beeker nodded thoughtfully. "So why stage that footage? Maybe they couldn't get a camera near the real factory, so, in the interest of expediency, they mocked up their own.''

"I don't think that plant there is a mock-up," Cowboy said, shaking his head. "I bet it's their money-maker.''

"Shipping their own product to finance the revolution?''

"They wouldn't be the first to justify their means with a noble end, you know," Cowboy said almost apologetically.

"I still ain't convinced they've got a noble end," Beeker grunted, watching Jackie and the general huddling like old buddies twenty paces ahead.

Back in the cave, they found Harry alertly on watch, while Rosie and Applebaum slept. Beeker set up a split-shift watch duty for the night, eight-hour shifts overlapping each other by four. That way, there'd always be two men on, one fresher than the other. After all the activity of the last couple of days, they could use with a long night's sleep. Tomorrow, Jackie would try to conduct her interview with some scrounged equipment, and hopefully by the next day they'd be on their way out of here.

Late afternoon was slipping into early evening. After seeing Jackie to bed, Beeker left Applebaum and Harry on watch, joining Rosie and Cowboy in sleep. As usual, it took no time at all for him to fall into a deep, dreamless slumber. He had no idea how long he stayed there. What seemed like moments later, he awoke to a savage firefight.

A flash-suppressed M-16 was barking loudly, the sound amplified to an almost deafening level by the cave walls.

It took him a second or two to come around. Sleep still clogged his head like a drug. He heard the *rat-tat-tat* of semi-auto AK fire and the hollow burping of a Schmeisser. Morales. There was shouting inside as Cowboy and Rosie leaped from slumber and groped for their weapons. Beeker dove for the cave entrance and slammed his M-16's hollow plastic stock hard against his shoulder.

Harry cursed loudly and spun away from the entrance. Blood jumped from his right shoulder. "I'm hit," he said calmly, as though stating a simple fact. He switched his rifle to his left hand, took his place again, and resumed firing. Beeker sprayed the darkness outside in an arc of three-round bursts. Ricochets caromed over their heads.

"Rosie," Beeker shouted over the noise of the firefight, "check that Jackie's okay."

There were scrambling noises behind him. Then silence,

"She's not here, Billy."

"*What*?"

Harry turned around. "She's out there, with Applebaum," he said.

"*What*?"

Harry said, "She woke up a while ago, had to go to the bathroom. Marty went with her. They must've been waiting for them."

"Shit*fuck*!"

Suddenly, the firing from outside ceased. Inside, the Black Berets held their fire and waited. Silence.

Then Morales's voice called out, "Beeker!"

"What is it, Morales?"

"I want you to come out of the cave in single file with your hands touching your heads. Leave your weapons in the cave. We will shoot anyone that doesn't do as we say."

148

"Why should we?"

Morales laughed. "Because I say so, Beeker. And because we have Miss Simmons and your man out here with guns pointed at their heads. Do you need any more reasons?"

"No, I suppose not," Beeker answered, lowering his forehead to rest against the M-16's carrying handle. "Shit," he said. "We fucking blew it." No one answered him.

# 11

"I blew it," Applebaum said, shrugging dejectedly.

The five Black Berets were back in the cave, minus Jackie, minus their weapons, and mighty pissed off.

"What happened?" Beeker asked.

Applebaum blotted a rising gash on his forehead with a gauze pad and said, "Middle of my watch, Jackie wakes up, has to go potty. I figured it was okay—I'd go with her to the latrine, Harry would hold things here. No problem. Motherfuckers were waiting for us, like they knew we was coming. Had me knocked down before I knew what was going on, and my weapon yanked before I could get near the trigger. Same slime-mold that had his eye on it this morning—it was Christmas for the bastard. They hustled Jackie off before I could even breathe." He stopped. "I coulda taken their weasel faces off if I'd'a been ready. I'm gonna even this score later—you just watch me."

Beeker looked at him evenly and said, "You should've woken me before going out." He left it at that. Inside, though, he didn't really know how he himself would've handled it. Two men to escort Jackie to the latrine? Wouldn't have made a difference, probably. An ambush was set up, and Jackie led Marty into it. Couldn't blame *him* for it. Could blame *her*, though. She had to have known it was coming, no doubt about it. Probably planned it earlier with Guiterrez. But why? Could she possibly be stupid enough to think she didn't need them? Had Guiterrez convinced her of that? What fantasyland was this woman living in?

"What next, Sarge?" Harry wanted to know, his right shoulder bandaged and his arm in a sling. Beeker shrugged and stared pensively at the ground.

"I don't think we should've given up our weapons," Rosie said flatly.

"I *know* we shouldn't have," Beeker shot back. "But when the enemy has one of your men, as well as the person you're supposed to be guarding, further resistance is foolish. We had to adjust to the new circumstances and play things accordingly. Forget what we should or shouldn't have done—concentrate on what we do *now*."

Rosie smiled respectfully. "You're right, of course, Beek. Sorry."

Applebaum put in, "I say we get our asses out of here and leave Jackie to rot." There were a couple of agreeing grunts.

Beeker shook his head. "Tempting but wrong, I think. We've got to take her out with us, whether she wants to go or not. We need to plan—" He was interrupted by the sound of footsteps on gravel.

"You need to plan *nothing*, my friends," Morales said triumphantly, walking into the cave. "As I told you before, you are all dead men. Plans at this point are futile." He was grinning at them smugly, his Schmeisser hung over his right shoulder on a jerry-rigged sling, muzzle to the ground and tubular metal stock tucked in behind the magazine box. Beeker briefly considered rushing him but stopped himself when he realized it was intended more to wipe the insulting look off the man's face than to accomplish anything practical. Definitely the wrong reason to act.

Instead he asked, "Where's Jackie?"

Morales's insipid smile grew wider. "The general is taking care of her. You shouldn't worry."

"What are you going to do with her?"

"Why, she'll be killed, of course, along with all of you."

No one said anything. Morales's delivery was so nonchalant, so casual, that it was obvious that death for all of them had been the plan from the beginning.

"What can you possibly gain?" Beeker asked him. "Killing six American citizens won't exactly endear you to the people of the United States."

"Señor Beeker, you underestimate us. Your deaths will be reported to the U.S. government—by us, of course—as the work of our ruthless military. Your bodies will be inhumanly mutilated and defiled." He seemed to particularly enjoy that part. "And while a journalist and her five-man 'camera crew' aren't as good as four nuns"—a laugh here—"there will no doubt be a great outcry in your country, led by Miss Simmons's fellow journalists. And after the evidence about the gutter politics of our poor country becomes known, can intervention here by U.S. powers be far behind? At the very least, we will get many U.S. dollars. Your country never needs much of an excuse to interfere in the affairs of others."

Beeker wasn't inclined right then to argue interventionist politics with the man—his mind was racing. "I get it," he said with a smile. "Of *course* this is no populist revolution—it's a goddamned drug war! Now that the drug trade has been restored here, you guys want in. What is it you're shooting for? Your piece as main manufacturers and exporters?"

"You think too small, my friend."

"The whole thing? Of course. Topple the military, install Guiterrez as president, and then kick all the foreign money-gobblers out of the country. Nationalize everything in sight, especially the cocaine trade. You'll have this place sewn up tight."

152

"Very good, Señor Beeker. How quickly you catch on. I must humbly admit you have our plan down *en totalidad*."

"And what'll you be—Guiterrez's vice-president and shoeshine boy?"

"No, I think I am in line to be commander-in-chief of all military forces, now that my predecessor has been taken back to France to face charges of certain atrocities he committed during World War II." His crooked smile left no doubt about who was responsible for *that* repatriation.

Beeker wanted to punch himself out. It all seemed crystal-clear now—something he should've seen from the very beginning. He knew there was no real way he could've known any of it, but that didn't make him feel any less stupid.

Abruptly, visiting hours were over. Morales called two names in the direction of the cave entrance. Two *nativo*-looking characters came in; wide, flat faces, almond-shaped eyes, and thick black hair cut around their heads like Moe of the Three Stooges. They were ageless—could've been anywhere between twenty and fifty—and looked tough in that stolid, passive, Indian way. Both had gleaming blue-metal Mini-Uzis in their hands, and held them like men accustomed to killing. Beeker could tell they knew how to use them.

Morales said a few sentences to them in an Indian language and then turned to the prisoners. He said, "These men will keep you company for the night. Have a restful sleep. It will be your last." Then he left.

The two guys—Beeker named them Moe and Larry—settled themselves between the cave entrance and the five Black Berets. They exchanged a few short sentences in their indecipherable Indian language, and then lapsed into a watchful silence, the tiny muzzles of their toylike Mini-Uzis never leaving the seated circle of five angry men. Not surprisingly, Beeker's conversational mood had passed.

"Sleep time," he announced after it was clear nothing was going to happen. "Let's spread out and get some rest while we can. We'll survey the situation tomorrow and play it from there."

They each found spots at different corners of the cave—making Moe and Larry's job more difficult—and curled themselves into sleeping positions. It wasn't the first time they'd faced a "certain" death sentence, and they knew from experience it was nothing to lose sleep over. If nothing had happened to turn things around by morning, they'd *make* something happen—and making something happen with a full night's sleep behind you was much preferable to doing it tired. Beeker close his eyes, relaxed his weary muscles, leveled his breathing rate, and was asleep.

And for the second time that night he was awakened by gunfire. They all jumped into sitting positions simultaneously and listened. The two Stooges were already alerted; one was in a combat crouch with his little Israeli lead-spitter held in two-handed readiness, the other checking the outside from a covered position by the cave entrance. These guys were well trained.

"Incoming mortars," Beeker said, his head cocked to take in the telltale sounds of approaching mortar and grenade ordnance. There was a chorus of whines, then a quick *WHUMPWHUMPWHUMP!* and the ground shook. Dirt drizzled from the cave ceiling.

"And copters." Cowboy added. Yes, Beeker could hear spinning rotors cutting the air. The sound of minigun fire, soon joined with *chumpchumping* anti-aircraft rounds, added to the now-deafening din.

"Shit," Rosie said, "we're being invaded!" He laughed.

Moe and Larry were rapidly losing their cool. All hell was breaking loose in the valley, and the two jokers couldn't decide if they should stay with their prisoners or

154

join the firefight. They needed someone to tell them what to do. Given the opportunity, Beeker would gladly make their minds up for them. He watched and waited.

The noise of battle grew louder. Men were shouting and running. Helicopters could be heard swooping in low, carpeting the valley with 7.62 minigun fire, 40mm grenade droppings, and 2.75-inch missiles. In the cave nobody moved. The *nativo* by the door was shouting now, pleading for instructions. He wanted to join the fight but was held back by his orders to watch the prisoners. The other one held his crouch, but his eyes were now drifting away from his prisoners, wanting desperately to see what was going on outside. Beeker watched the man's black pupils yo-yo back and forth, waiting for an opening. The others, though looking relaxed, were poised for his signal.

The moment came. The guy's eyes left his charges for one split-second too many. Beeker blinked hard, and that was it.

Harry and Marty launched themselves at the guard by the door; the other three went for the one facing them. Beeker's big hands closed over the little 14 ½-inch submachine gun and pushed up, spraying the ceiling with 9mm rounds. Rosie's muscular left arm lassoed the guy's neck and whipped his head back with a snap. Cowboy's shoulders impacted with the soft bone just below the man's kneecaps, and buckled both legs in the wrong direction. The man was out.

The guard by the door heard his buddy's weapon fire and started to spin around. He was one-third into it when Harry's stiffened fingers jabbed the little bundle of nerves in the hollow at the base of his skull. He twitched like a jerked puppet and started to go down. Harry caught him around the neck with his still-good left arm and pulled back hard on his chin, snapping his neck. Marty's right hand had clamped down on the receiver port of the man's weapon, just an inch forward of the rear sight. With his left hand he chopped at the man's wrist, forcing him to release his grip. The Mini-Uzi was his, still unfired.

While Beeker and Harry crouched by the cave entrance, the three others dragged the bodies back and dumped them into the shower stall. Outside it was like the end of the world, which, of course, they'd all seen a few dozen times before. The camp's electric lights were gone; the only illumination now came from the strobe-lighting explosions, sparking muzzle flashes from hundreds of automatic rifles, and multicolored tracer threads streaming through the air like fountains at a water show. God only knew if anyone out there could see what they were shooting at.

Marty came up, leaned his head out over Beeker's, and whooped with delight. "All *right*! Fireworks!" The boy was finally in his element.

"Calm down, Applebaum," Beeker said with mock sternness. "No time to enjoy the floor show. Looks like the Army is here to clean this place up, and I don't fancy getting caught in the crossfire. Let's get over to the general's big house, snatch him and Jackie, and get the hell out of here. Knowing hotshot revolutionary leaders, I'm sure the guy's got an escape route set up for himself. I plan on us making use of it. Let's *move*!"

They ran from the mouth of the cave, one by one, in a low crouch, keeping to the darkness. They moved steadily toward the back end of the valley, leapfrogging around each other, alert for incoming ordnance and other people—be they guardsmen or guerrillas. But they didn't encounter much human traffic at all. By this time, everyone seemed to be in position already, and the brunt of the action was concentrated at the valley's main entrance and over by the drug factory. Evidently, Army helicopters were dropping troopers at those two points.

In all, the Black Berets' path crossed with those of ten

156

of Guiterrez's men along the way. None of them survived. The first was a group of three, running exhaustedly, their assault rifles held in present-arms across their chests. They were tripped and overpowered immediately, and dispatched with point-blank bursts from the Mini-Uzis. Their weapons—three spanking-new AKMs, the Soviet-made successor to the venerable '47—were collected, and several plastic banana-clip magazines were removed from the dead men's web-belts and stuffed into pockets. They were now all armed.

Not surprisingly, the headquarters building was a bee-hive of activity. Though all the windows were shrouded in blackout curtains, they could see bright lights burning inside. The front door kept banging open, shooting a shaft of white light into the darkness, then disgorging running figures. There seemed to be more figures leaving than coming; in fact, after a few minutes' wait, it looked like *everybody* was leaving.

When the exiting activity slackened, Beeker gave the order to move in. He took the lead with Rosie, leaping up onto the building's wooden porch and pausing for a split second on the opposite side of the front door from Boone. Beeker, on the knob side, spun in front of and kicked it open while Rosie sprayed the open doorway with full-auto AKM fire. He emptied a thirty-round clip into the room at waist level, cutting three men in half. They screamed and toppled over, blood watering their trousers.

The magazine exhausted, he punched the release in preparation for a reload. Beeker meanwhile leaped into the room from behind him, Mini-Uzi in firing position, weight balanced on the balls of his feet. His eyes and weapon did a parallel scan of the room, and after satisfying himself that all occupants were dead, he ran forward and kicked in the next door. Two short bursts of Schmeisser fire greeted him, aimed for the chest of someone standing in the

157

middle of the doorway. But Beeker had pulled back after kicking the door, and the slugs slapped harmlessly into the far wall. He peeked the Mini-Uzi around the doorjamb with his left hand and sprayed the room low with three seconds of full-auto. He heard Morales scream and fall.

Rosie jumped around him and into the room. Beeker followed and saw Morales sprawled behind a bed, his face riddled with bullets. Obviously, the man had been interrupted: There was a leather syringe case zipped open and laid out on the bed. Next to it was a fully loaded works ready for injection. The man was spiking up for battle. Wouldn't need it now.

The room's other door opened onto the hallway that ran the length of the house. Applebaum, the bloody gauze pad falling from his forehead, was leading the wall-hugging sideways crab-shuffle toward the operations room in the rear. When they got there, Harry kicked the door in while Cowboy opened up with his AKM. The room was empty. Where was the general? Certainly not leading his troops. Probably packing his bags.

"Bedroom!" he shouted, and instantly Rosie and Cowboy ran for the hall leading to Guiterrez's private quarters. Behind them, Harry and Marty were doing a room-by-room no-knock. Kick and shoot. Noisy, fun, and effective. They were having a high old time.

They reached the door to Guiterrez's bedroom and could hear scrambling noises from behind it. Beeker motioned Rosie and Cowboy aside and then rammed the door with his boot heel. It flew open. They hung back, expecting gunfire, but none came. Instead . . .

"*No hace fuego!*" Guiterrez's trembling voice came from inside. He was begging them not to shoot. "*Por favor, por favor,*" he pleaded. "*Yo tengo mucho dinero.*" Now he was telling them he had lots of money. The guy presumed they were the Army, and he was hoping to buy his way out. He was out of luck.

Beeker called out: "I want everybody in the room face-down in the middle of the floor, with their legs and arms spread. I want to see no weapons and no one standing. You have three seconds!"

"You!" Guiterrez was incredulous.

"I said three seconds!" Beeker shouted again. "Starting *now*! One—two—three!" There was a scramble. Beeker poked the submachine gun around the molding and arced the room with a chest-high, full-auto burst. When the magazine clicked empty, Rosie went in low, firing off three quick single-rounders. Beeker saw him get to his feet laughing.

"Hey, Sarge, Cowboy, come look what we got in here!"

Beeker slipped in, the pilot at his heels. Guiterrez and Jackie, both half-dressed, were laid out on the floor, shaking. The bed was a mess. Like Morales, they too had been interrupted—they'd been fucking when the Army attack had come.

"I bet you two felt the earth move that time, eh?" Rosie couldn't keep himself from laughing. Jackie was beginning to blush, her embarrassment overcoming her fear. Even her two cute buttocks were turning red.

Beeker went down on one knee next to the general, who was practically in tears. He put the stumpy muzzle of his Mini-Uzi to the guy's temple and chambered the first round of a fresh clip.

"Not cut out for the active life, are you, General?" He said mockingly. Guiterrez did nothing but continue whimpering.

"Well, now, seeing as we're all here and the atmosphere outside is distinctly unhealthy, I say we get out *quick*. Don't you agree, General?" Guiterrez nodded his head. "And I've got me a notion in that you got yourself a

159

nice, easy escape hatch for your own personal use, just for occasions such as this. Am I right there, General?" It was slower in coming this time, but there was another nod. "Good, I thought so. Now, what do you say you pack up some of that money you were tellin' us about earlier, and some of that evidence you showed us, and then lead us out of here?"

"Already packed," he said into the floor. Beeker followed his eyes to a dressing table on the other side of the big double bed. Sitting there was a leather briefcase. It was closed but bulging its seams.

"Now ain't that convenient," he said with a sarcastic smile. "So now all you have to do is cover your shameful nakedness and get us out of here." His tone abruptly changed. "On your feet!" He ordered them. "Get dressed, *now*!" They jumped.

The escape route started with a tunnel in the basement of the headquarters building, pointing in the direction of the huge mountain that formed the valley fortress's back wall. Beeker pushed Guiterrez into the uncovered hole, the first to lead the way, following him with his weapon ready. Behind him came Rosie, then Jackie, Cowboy, Harry, and Applebaum. It was a low tunnel—only about three feet tall at its highest—and they had to go through it on their hands and knees. It took a good ten minutes for them all to come through, the ground shaking with the booming of nearby explosions the entire time.

The tunnel ended in a tall chamber with a ladder going up. It took them about twelve feet above to a cave with a ceiling tall enough for them to stand up straight with no trouble. Guiterrez pointed a direction, and Beeker prodded him with his Mini-Uzi to get him moving. The cave wound up and out, lit sporadically by the flashlights they'd taken from the headquarters building's supply stock. The

160

cave mouth was covered with vines and leafy vegetation, and they had to rip the stuff away in order to pull themselves out into the air.

It was dawn, and dead quiet. A few birds cawed to each other, and occasionally a monkey chittered to its mate, but otherwise everything was silent. Had the attack finished, or was the mountain between them and the battle baffling the sound?

Beeker looked around him. They were on a relatively level shoulder of the mountain, two-thirds of the way down into another densely forested jungle valley. The sun was rising into a clear sky, the few wisps of puffy white clouds burning off into vapor before their eyes. It was a tranquil scene. Beeker turned to Guiterrez.

"And now?"

The general pointed with his chin. "Over there," he said.

They all looked. At the edge of the clearing was something—a very large something—covered with a camo tarp. Beeker went over and pulled up an edge to see what was underneath. It was a Huey. He smiled.

"A fucking helicopter!" Cowboy said, standing at Beeker's elbow. He shook his head with amazement. "The General's stashed himself a fucking helicopter. I do hope the thing's gassed up and ready to go. . . ."

It was, of course.

# 12

---

"And what do you intend to do with me, Mr. Beeker?"
Guiterrez didn't say it like he was worried, just curious.
Obviously, he knew that—as they say—the jig was up.

"Not rightly sure yet, General. Probably trade you off
to the Army for safe conduct out of here, if they're buying."
Beeker shrugged. He was telling the truth; he wasn't sure.
That's why, after flying fifteen or twenty miles due west
into the mountains, he had started looking for someplace
to put down. He needed time to rest up and think.

They spotted a likely LZ soon enough. More ancient
Inca ruins apparently—an overgrown shelf-terraced hillside,
with a thin path leading downward to a stoned-in cave.
According to Guiterrez it probably had been a tomb for a
member of some royal family. They tarped over the Huey so
it'd be tough to spot from the air, and trooped down into the
cave. Jackie, who hadn't said a word to anyone the entire
time, went immediately to sleep. The rest of them dipped
into the canned rations stashed in the copter's storage
well.

"I can't believe it," Cowboy muttered, holding up a
dented can of ham and lima beans. "Beans and motherfuckers—haven't eaten any of this slop in ten years."

Rosie laughed. "And how much you wanna bet they
taste just as lousy as you remember?" No one argued.

Beeker tossed the empty ration can aside. "So, General,"

he asked Guiterrez, "how much *dinero* you put in that bag?"

The man shrugged insincerely. "I don't stop to count it, Mr. Beeker. Somewhere between thirty and fifty thousand American dollars, I would guess. With a few thousand more in various other currencies. It was all I had near at hand."

"No chance to dip into the real stash, eh?" Rosie needled him.

Beeker said, "So you've got access to a lot more, then?"

"Why do you wish to know this? Do you plan to squeeze as much as you can out of me?"

"Relax, General. We may be mercenaries, but we're not kidnappers or extortionists, though I can't think of anyone who deserves it more than you. No, I'm just sizing up our assets here, in case we have some hard bargaining to do. Answer my question—you have access to more?"

"Yes," he said reluctantly. "With the aid of international communication, I could obtain more."

"From where?" Beeker kept pushing.

"Switzerland and the Caribbean. Must I submit to this third degree?"

"Yes. How much?"

"Unlimited."

"Where's your source, Guiterrez? You couldn't be the top of this organization; it's too big, and you're small potatoes. Who's in charge of this outfit?"

Guiterrez didn't answer at first. Beeker could read clearly the debate going on inside in the man's eyes? Lie? Truth? Somewhere in between? Then suddenly, the man just shrugged with resignation, as though he had nothing to lose, and Beeker knew he'd be getting the truth.

"An American businessman, with the assistance of some of his associates, put this operation together and runs it.

163

He is a very shrewd and powerful man, I must tell you—no, *warn* you. If you try to take him on or just annoy him in any way—''

''Where is he now?'' Beeker asked, ignoring the threat.

''He owns an island in the Bahamas group, called Stagg's Cay—''

Cowboy interrupted. ''Vanesto! Robert Vanesto!''

Beeker said, ''Who?''

''You remember, Billy—he ran an investment scam, made millions and then took a fall. He tried to buy his way out with a huge contribution to Tricky Dick's '72 campaign. And when that blew up in his face, he hit the road and has been living on the run around the Caribbean ever since. He controls a healthy hunk of the south-to-north coke trade, using Stagg's Cay as his transshipment point.''

Guiterrez said nothing, but Beeker knew Cowboy's facts were reliable. Billy shook his head disgustedly. ''It's amazing what scum rises to the top in this business, isn't it?''

''It is potentially the most profitable commodity on the world market today,'' Guiterrez said, like a stockbroker talking about frozen pork bellies.

''Great, but I'll wait until it hits the big board before I buy my shares,'' Beeker answered. ''At least we know what we're up against now and what kind of resources our guest here can draw on if we need it. How much do you think you're worth to Mr. Vanesto, General?''

''Right now?'' He dropped his shoulders. ''Who's to tell? What good is a general without an army?'' No one answered him—or offered any sympathy, either.

Beeker turned to Cowboy again and said, ''You want to give me a hand with something up by the chopper?'' They left Rosie in charge of the general—not that he really needed watching— and headed up the path to the shrouded Huey.

''You got a plan, Sarge?''

Beeker shook his head. "Not really. I'm just going to hail the commander of that raiding party on the bird's radio, and see if we can parley."

The man in question—Colonel Escojedo, as he identified himself—didn't much like the idea, but consented grudgingly. He agreed to let them fly into the now-government-controlled valley for a face-to-face, emphasizing that he promised nothing. Beeker signed off and returned with Cowboy to the cave down below.

Rosie jumped at the guy's name. "Escojedo? Did he leave a first name?"

"No," Beeker said, "why?"

"I trained a kid named Esteban Escojedo when I did my instructor year at Bragg in sixty-eight, sixty-nine. Can't quite remember, but I'll bet he was Peruvian, and he's our man here."

"How'd you two get on?"

"Fine—he was a great kid. Smart, strong, and honest; one of the best I ever trained."

Beeker felt a ray of hope poke through the heavy cloud cover overshadowing his spirits. "Why don't you come along with me and Cowboy, Rosie, and if it's the same guy, you can slap each other on the back and talk about old times."

"You bet, boss—and maybe I can con him into lettin' us outta here with our skins intact."

Cowboy took the general's Huey the long way around. He put a few extra mountains on the route between their ground position and the valley fortress, so government choppers wouldn't be swarming all over the place as soon as they touched down to talk. Their final approach was slow and high, Cowboy dropping them feather-light on the ridge where they'd first laid eyes on the fortress yesterday morning.

165

A couple of M-16-armed troopers were waiting for them when they got out.

"*Vaya conmigo*," one of them said, and led Beeker and Rosie directly to Guiterrez's old headquarters building. In the general's old office, Colonel Escojedo waited, sitting ramrod straight behind the desk, red beret poised on his shaved scalp, a thick black Vandyke beard circling his mouth. He stood up at attention and bowed slightly from the waist.

"Mr. Beeker."

"Hello, Colonel. This is my associate, Roosevelt Boone."

The Colonel's dark eyes swung in Rosie's direction. The eyes narrowed, and the bushy brows lowered. "Boone?" he said.

"I believe the Colonel and I have met, Beek. How are you Esteban?"

The colonel's face broke into a grin. "Sergeant Boone!" Beeker let out a breath of relief; the man was honestly happy to see Rosie. The two shook hands and punched each other's arms, like old frat buddies.

"Now tell me," the colonel said after a while. "What in hell are you doing *here*, and what's your involvement with this *maricon* Guiterrez?"

Rosie shook his head. "It's a long, stupid story, my man."

Escojedo flipped up his hands. "I've got plenty of time, *amigo*. Tell me." Though delivered with a friendly tone, it wasn't just a request—it was an order.

Rosie gave him the economy version of the story. "So you see," he wrapped it up, "we've got nothing to do with Guiterrez per se, just safeguarding someone who's visiting him."

The Colonel gave a sad laugh. "From decorated Green Beret to mercenary—quite a comedown, Sergeant."

"Call me Rosie," he said, shrugging it off. "I think it's

166

more of a promotion, actually. The pay's a damn sight better, and I get to say no when I please. Don't sound like a comedown to me.''

Escojedo smiled, not uncharitably. "I understand. I wish I had the luxury to say no now and again. I am afflicted with a particularly unpleasant commanding officer, but soldiers are not granted the privilege of picking their superiors. But, so much for small talk. Now, I'm afraid, we must get down to the issue at hand: What is it you wish to talk with me about?''

"Our skins,'' Beeker said bluntly.

"In exchange for what?''

"Guiterrez.''

"Your lives for his?''

"Basically, yeah. I want your assurance that once you have Guiterrez, my men and I, along with our charge, will be safely put aboard a plane back to the States.''

"Frankly, it doesn't sound as if you're offering me very much. Guiterrez is effectively a nonentity, a dead man. Whether you hand him over to us, or we hunt him down and kill him in the mountains—and we've proven our ability to do that—it's all the same to us. It's a matter of time, really. You're not giving us anything we don't already have.''

"What can you gain by keeping us?''

Escojedo shrugged. "My orders are clear. I'm to detain you pending the arrival of Brigadier Alomar, the Defense Minister.''

Rosie and Beeker exchanged looks. Alomar was a major player in Guiterrez's film. It was time to roll in the heavy artillery.

"Colonel,'' Beeker began, "what do you know about the cocaine trade in this country?''

"I know that it is big business, and pigs like Guiterrez are trying—under the guise of revolution—to make it bigger.

167

Our government is doing what it can to control it, but our resources are meager. What more can I say?"

Escojedo looked like he believed what he was saying, so he was either a good liar or completely in the dark about the reality of the situation. It was time for the sucker punch. Beeker delivered it.

"What if I told you that I could supply you with evidence that your Defense Minister, Brigadier Alomar, along with all the top officials of the military government, are in league with various foreign and domestic influences to expand the drug traffic in Peru, and share in the profits?"

The colonel's eyes widened. "Officially, I would say you were a liar and a traitor to my country. Unofficially"— he paused to choose his words carefully—"unofficially, I would say show me your evidence and let me see for myself. You see, Señor Beeker, I am not without eyes and ears and a nose—and all of them have, at one time or another, told me that I know only a small part of the truth. Generals with expensive jewelry, homes filled with art treasures, huge plantations in the mountains—there is indeed something dishonest going on. I would say show me, Señor Beeker."

"Does that make our deal any more worthwhile?"

"Hard for me to say that now, before seeing anything. But if what you claim is true, it may make fulfilling my side of the bargain more difficult. You see what I mean?"

"Sure. The question is, would you even try?" Beeker heard Rosie shift uncomfortably in his seat. He was treading on thin ice here.

"That was either a very courageous, or very stupid thing, to say, Mr. Beeker." Escojedo's face was impassive.

"Getting to the truth sometimes takes both courage and stupidity, Colonel." Beeker watched him.

"Quite true," the man said with a growing smile. "Let me say this, then—if, after I've examined what you have

168

to show me, I decide that what you say is true, I will then try my best to get you and your party out of Peru. The accommodations might not be first class, and the route back to the *Estados Unidos* might not be a direct one, but you have my word that I will get you out. Is that good enough?''

Beeker nodded. ''Rosie tells me you're an honorable man. That's good enough for me.'' They both got up and shook hands.

''Excellent. Now, I suggest we have a drink and decide on a mutually agreeable time and location where I can inspect your evidence. Then, you must leave here before the brigadier and his butcher squad arrive. It would be, I suspect, a most unpleasant meeting.'' He laughed knowingly.

The colonel was convinced. He had taken a long time to study the contents of Guiterrez's briefcase, now bulging considerably less without the bundles of money cluttering it up. He looked at the film first, holding it up to the sun for light, using a magnifying glass when he needed to see more detail—faces, words, etc. Then Beeker showed him the actual documents—the contracts, bank statements, etc., that Guiterrez had featured in his film. He looked at them all thoroughly and, when he was through, looked up at Beeker and Rosie. He seemed suddenly tired.

''Some of this is bullshit,'' he said, holding up a fistful of paper. ''Forgeries, lies, or merely inconclusive. But most of it, unfortunately, tells a very ugly story—a story that I must believe.'' He paused and looked off into the distant mountains, beyond his helicopter that sat quiet nearby. The fatigue on his face turned into anger. ''These vultures are picking the bones of my country clean. They must be stopped—''

''Forgive me, Colonel,'' Beeker said with uncharacteristic politeness, ''but you and what army? This won't be just a

169

matter of calling up the local newspapers or having a new election. This corruption pervades your government and military, so you couldn't even change it by just knocking off a president or a general. Nothing short of a civil war would do it at this point.''

"You think I am unaware of that, Señor Beeker? I know only too well the consequences of what I am contemplating. But I have no choice. What else am I to do? Acquiesce? Play along? Ask to be included? I would rather die!'' He clenched his fist and crumpled the papers.

"You probably will,'' Beeker said with some sympathy. "But I understand only too well why you must choose that course. I'm sure I'd do the same damn thing if I were in your shoes. Thank God I'm not. My grandmother once told me an old Cherokee saying when I was a kid. It went something like, 'How can you expect to soar with eagles if you dance with turkeys?' I don't think either of us, Colonel, were cut out for hanging with turkeys.''

Escojedo laughed appreciatively. "I suspect you are right, my friend. But soaring with eagles seems so far from our grasp. What's left for us?''

"Got me, Colonel. I just want to be able to sleep at night.''

Rosie asked, "Is there anything we could do to help you out, Esteban?''

"I'm sorry you asked that, Rosie,'' Escojedo answered after a thoughtful pause. "Because indeed there is something you can do for me. Kill Brigadier Alomar.''

Rosie choked. "Now hold it, Esteban, we ain't hired assassins, you know. And we don't give it away free, either. We can't just stroll in to your camp and off this old guy for you.''

"I don't want to have to do this, but I am now renegotiating the terms of our agreement. The price of your freedom now includes the death of my commanding officer.''

170

"Shit, man, you're *serious*." Rosie cried out. "I can't fucking believe it!"

"Do believe it, my friend. Alomar is the iron grip that holds my people by the neck. He must be eliminated. It is a job that must be done, and it must be done by an outsider. I don't think I could bring myself to do it, as certain as I am that the old fool deserves it. And, besides, my men must never connect me with the killing. If an outsider does it, we blame it on the cocaine. Once Alomar and his personal commando squad are eliminated, I know my men will follow me."

"Now hold it, Esteban!" Rosie was growing visibly panicked. "The job has suddenly grown—now it's not only the fucking general, but his damn crew of bodyguards, too? Jesus! We're mass murderers? I can't believe you're asking us to do this."

The colonel said nothing more. He just stared at them. Then Beeker said, "It's a deal."

"*What?*" Rosie was beside himself. "What you saying, Billy? You gone crazy? We can't just waltz into their camp and grease all these guys! We'll get our asses toasted for sure!"

Beeker ignored him, but inside a voice was saying, "*Some good has to come out of this whole fiasco.*" To Escojedo he said, "Get out your maps. I want you to leave me a sniper rifle and at least a dozen rounds of ammunition right here." He pointed to a spot on the colonel's chart on the ridge overlooking the back end of the valley, just behind the camp's headquarters structure. "A night sight for the rifle, if one is available," he added. Escojedo nodded. "Then I want you to make sure Alomar and his men sleep in this building tonight." He indicated Guiterrez's command house. "Keep anyone you want alive at least a few hundred yards away from there, more if they have

171

skin that tans easily. Be prepared for some fireworks at around midnight or so.''

Escojedo smiled and nodded his head. ''My men and I will be ready. And I guarantee that you will be in Bolivia by noon tomorrow. I have already arranged it.''

Rosie was shaking his head back and forth and looking up to the sky. ''I can't believe either of you guys.'' He walked back to the Huey, muttering to himself.

Beeker found the rifle, wrapped in a blanket under a pile of loose brush, exactly where he'd asked Escojedo to leave it. He shouldered the bundle and climbed back up to the top of the ridge, over which he'd just come. His watch read eleven thirty-five when he reached the spot that he had scouted earlier as a firing position. The *chachacomo* trees thinned out to almost nothing up here, and brown scrub grass clung to the dusty earth in tenacious patches. A bright moon shone through the patchy cloud cover. Beeker's measured breathing was the only sound in the night.

He lay the blanket-wrapped sniper rifle down and surveyed his target area. It was a good thirteen hundred yards away, more like eighteen hundred once you figured in the effect gravity would have on the downward traveling projectile. It was going to be a tough shot. He hoped the rifle was up to it. He knew he was.

He turned his attention to the bundle and opened the blanket. He couldn't believe what he saw. Blackly handsome, cradled in the woolen folds of the blanket, was a sweetheart weapon—a Heckler & Koch PSG-1 Counter-Sniper rifle. It was an incredibly accurate, semi-automatic weapon with a twenty-round magazine box, a twenty-five-and-a-half-inch bull barrel, and a 6 x 42 Hensoldt Wetzlar telescopic sight that illuminated its cross hairs for you in low light. He hefted it gently by its plastic-coated stock, which adjusted to fit any shoulder, and settled its nearly

172

eighteen pounds into place. Sighting along its forty-eight-inch total length, he smiled. It felt great, like dropping your butt onto the saddle of a competition Harley. This weapon has *balls*, Billy thought.

It was time to set up. Eleven forty-five. Applebaum would be coming up through the tunnel in the basement by now. He lay down on the ground and set the rifle into its collapsible tripod. He adjusted the ergonomic wooden handle to fit his grip and then screwed the cheek plate atop the stock until it fit nicely against his face. Removing the rubber lens guards from the telescope, he began sweeping the target area, looking for the lit windows of the command cabin.

He found them soon enough, made the necessary range and elevation adjustments—handled almost automatically by the rifle's inboard systems—and settled in to wait.

At precisely twelve o'clock, Beeker heard a muffled explosion from the valley below. The command structure shook and then spit out all its basement windows. Smoke followed and then the first tentative lickings of orange flame. Billy loosened his right arm and shoulder muscles, wiped the sweat from his palm, and encircled the pistol grip and trigger with his hand. He pushed the illuminated cross-hairs activator button on the left side of the sight—giving him two minutes of light—and drew a bead on the cabin's back door.

With a bang it burst open, and men in baggy military-issue underwear came out at a stumbling run. They were shouting, "*Fuego! Fuego!*" in desperate voices, coughing and spitting. Depend on Applebaum to spark a good fire.

Beeker waited until a fat old man, his gray hair in wild disarray, cleared the door before he started firing. The gut-bulging general got it first, the 7.62mm slug piercing his naked chest just to the left of his breastbone. It passed diagonally through his chest cavity rupturing the right

173

ventricle of his already overtaxed heart, and exited his body just below his left shoulder blade. He was dead before the lead hit the ground behind him.

The rifle's near-total lack of recoil allowed him to squeeze off five more rounds in quick succession. One for each man standing dumbly on the grass, wondering what was going on. Now five dead men wondering nothing. He scanned the area around the cabin for the other men in the squad but saw no one. The building was burning brightly now, and from the screams emerging from it, Beeker surmised the others hadn't made it out. Saved him the trouble.

He gave it another minute. When nothing more happened, he got up, brushed himself off, and walked away from there. Cowboy and Applebaum would be waiting in the Huey on the other side of the mountain. He headed down the path.

Shame he had to leave the rifle, though. It was a nice piece. But there'd be others.